Ride 'Em

Delphine Dryden

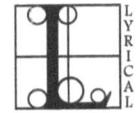

LYRICAL PRESS
Kensington Publishing Corp.
www.kensingtonbooks.com

LYRICAL PRESS BOOKS are published by

Kensington Publishing Corp.
119 West 40th Street
New York, NY 10018

All Kensington titles, imprints, and distributed lines are available at special quantity discounts for bulk purchases for sales promotion, premiums, fund-raising, educational, or institutional use.

Special book excerpts or customized printings can also be created to fit specific needs. For details, write or phone the office of the Kensington Sales Manager: Kensington Publishing Corp., 119 West 40th Street, New York, NY 10018. Attn. Sales Department. Phone: 1-800-221-2647.

Lyrical Press and Lyrical Press logo Reg. U.S. Pat. & TM Off.

First Electronic Edition: July 2016
eISBN-13: 978-1-60183-675-5
eISBN-10: 1-60183-675-9

First Print Edition: July 2016
ISBN-13: 978-1-60183-676-2
ISBN-10: 1-60183-676-7

Printed in the United States of America

Acknowledgments

So many thanks to my far-flung support network, for seeing me through and getting my writing motor revved again. To Christine d'Abo, Shari Slade, and Kailynn Jones, for all the online and in-person encouragement—and for making me remember that my friendships can help me be stronger than my depression. To Elisabeth Blackwell, for suddenly always being there, sharing a brain with me in the most delightful and unexpected way. To my wonderful family. To my amazing agent, Courtney Miller-Callihan (no idea why she hasn't given up on me yet, but I'm so thrilled she's hanging in there and being so awesome). And to the whole team at Kensington, but particularly Esi, for helping make my kinky dude ranch come to life!

Chapter One

Logan got up early that Friday, just to see the sunrise. He needed it that morning, more than most. A little quiet time with the old homestead at its most beautiful, fresh with the unspoiled promise of spring. A fine shimmer of dew still coated the broad swath of lawn spreading out below the porch of the ranch house, and the scattered clouds appeared to linger on the horizon for the sole purpose of holding the outlandish dawn colors a few minutes longer.

From this vantage point, the drive leading to the house seemed to drop sheer away about a quarter mile out. Perspective and the haze of morning made a floating island of the hilltop, and Logan wished he could keep it that way. In the distance, misty rises studded with limestone outcroppings marched away in successively darker ranks. Close by, there was only the house and the hill, and the man who still couldn't quite believe he owned them now.

A rooster crowed from over near the barn, hoarse and grumpy. Like a reflex, Logan checked his mental list. Had he assigned anyone to gather the eggs yet? He couldn't immediately recall. He'd been doing it himself but would happily hand the chore over to somebody else. Logan had never been a big fan of chickens. The hens were okay, but the damn cranky rooster always went straight for his ankles as soon as he entered the pen. He had a new sympathy for masochists, but it only served to reinforce how very much he wasn't one. Not his kink, not his kink at all.

Masochists. Ah. *Diego.* He'd foisted the job off on Diego as part of "gamekeeping," he recalled, brightening a bit. And since Diego, along with the rest of the staff, would be showing up for work in a few hours, Logan didn't have much more time to himself. Once the guests arrived that evening, he'd have no time at all. He turned his attention back to the sunrise, only to find the moment had passed him by. Only a faint tint of lavender remained near the horizon, fading into the plumbago blue of the rest of the sky.

Sighing, he knocked back the last of his industrial-strength coffee and jumped down from the porch rail where he'd been perched. He used the garden hose to rinse the cup, then set it on the steps and headed for the barn. He still had at least a few hours' worth of chores to do before he could justify saddling his horse, Charley, up for some exercise.

As a kid, Logan had never appreciated how much work his grandparents put into running Hilltop Ranch as a vacation spot, or really understood why his father had decided to close down the guest cottages and all but abandon the place except for weekend hunting trips. Now Logan got it, but it was too late to reconsider his decision to reopen the ranch to visitors. He'd burned his bridges, leaving his job in Houston and selling his house there in order to help finance the buyout of the ranch from his parents. His brother and cousin had gone in with him, but both of them had kept their day jobs. Logan hadn't wanted to leave himself a way to cop out. This commitment was for the long haul, but he was only beginning to realize the magnitude of what he was in for.

Running the guest ranch was like managing a hunting lodge, stable, bed-and-breakfast, and a sleepaway camp, all at the same time. He had Robert to cook and deal with the laundry, Diego to keep track of the game and help out with maintenance, and Lamar overseeing the stables, but Logan felt the pressure of entertaining the guests squarely on his own shoulders. As it should be—he had taken it on himself to be the man in charge, to finally own that role in every sense of the word instead of just in the bedroom or at the kink club. But this was an awful lot of hospitality. It wasn't enough for the guests to enjoy the stay, either. They had to want to come back. They had to want to tell their friends. If he didn't get some word of mouth going, he was screwed, because he was all out of financial padding. He'd been late on two note payments already, juggling funds and shifting other bills around to try to stretch his funds, and his loan officer was breathing down his neck. This week *had* to be a success.

"It's a big job, isn't it, Charley?" he asked the big dappled gray gelding as they ambled back toward the barnyard after a long ride across the property, touring the two most likely spots for the upcoming turkey hunt. "Isn't it?"

The horse nodded his head, and Logan chuckled at his noble steed.

"You're my ace in the hole, Charley. A born showman."

His chuckle was echoed by a raspier one from the shadow of the barn door. A leathery, bearded face emerged from the gloom as Logan and Charley entered the building.

"He's a ham, all right," Lamar agreed, reaching out to take Charley's reins. "Is he gonna help you meet and greet?"

"Of course," Logan said, dismounting. "You might want to walk him a bit. We had a good jog out there, and damn, but it's already getting hot for March."

"Weatherman said it'd get up past eighty. You should know better. He'll need a wash if he's going to be seen by his adoring public." The grizzled old man swept a dubious glance up and down Logan's sweaty form. "You, too."

"Aw, do I hafta?"

"Don't think you're too big for me to take a switch to, boy."

Lamar and Logan grinned at each other in perfect accord. The old hand had practically raised Logan, who'd spent as much time in the barn growing up as he had in the house or at school. Lamar had been openly skeptical about Logan's grand scheme to reopen the guest ranch. But he'd agreed to stay on, and Logan knew how much his loyalty was worth. What's more, he'd actually learned from Lamar how to cut a switch and use it—not that the old man had any idea Logan still sometimes used that knowledge in an altogether different context.

"It's after three now, and people'll start showing up around four, so no time for a shower. But I'll hose myself down and put on a clean shirt, if that'll make you happy, old man."

"I s'pose it'll have to do. C'mon, Charley."

Logan started for the faucet on the side of the barn, then changed his mind and headed back toward the main house, remembering that he'd left the hose unwound on the front porch that morning after cleaning his mug with it. Might as well use it one more time before tidying it away.

* * *

Mindy Valek knew the road from Dallas to Bolero like the back of her hand. The unattractive part of her hand, with the weird patch of freckles and the little moon-shaped scar from that one time she was ironing a shirt and the hot iron fell over on her knuckle. She'd given up on ironing after that but the scar remained, a reminder perhaps that she needed to stop trying so hard to impress. Or maybe just that having her work clothes professionally cleaned and pressed was worth every penny. Ironic that she'd packed only jeans and casual tops for this week, when it was more important than ever that she make a good impression to get the job done.

Vacation, she told herself. *You're paying for this week.*

She was really paying for the opportunity. The chance to talk Logan Hill into leasing the mineral rights to his new property. His grandparents had refused when they owned the land. His parents had refused. But Mindy's boss—and stepfather—Bud Jameson only cared about the current owner's refusal, and Mindy was determined to succeed where others had failed. It was probably the only thing that could help her survive her company's brutal cutbacks and keep her job, keep *herself*, afloat without compromising any more of her independence to nepotism.

That was the arrangement she'd made with Bud back when she'd taken the job, too tempted by his offer to refuse. He'd tried to give her a signing bonus; she'd insisted on using it to pay him back for helping her with her college tuition. He'd still been the shiny new stepdad then, the nice guy who'd rescued her mom from post-divorce poverty and elevated her into a world of oil money, society columns, charity balls, and spa treatments. Mindy had accepted the tuition help, at her mother's insistence, but had felt a tremendous sense of relief when the obligation was paid back. And now that she worked for Bud, and knew the flip side of his character, she was glad not to be any more beholden to him than she had to be.

She'd insisted on being treated like any other employee . . . and he'd honored her wish, because he was ethical when it came to family. But when it came to business, there was no velvet glove on the ruthless iron fist. Bud was a crusher of souls, a destroyer of dreams, and if he hadn't been the CEO of the biggest land services outfit in Texas, Mindy would have hightailed it out of his office within six months of arriving there.

That had been during a mini-boom, when there were multiple offers to choose from. Now things were sliding into bust again, and without this deal she knew she was doomed in the next round of lay-offs—and in the current job market she had no hope of finding another position in time to avoid losing her car, her condo, and the meager savings she'd been able to amass while still repaying the student loans she'd taken out before Bud's white-knight arrival on the scene. And if she thwarted Bud, he wouldn't make finding a new job any easier. She needed this deal like she'd never needed one before.

The price? One week at a tourist-trap "guest ranch" just outside the town her mother had worked so hard to get her out of. And possibly the cost of a little self-respect, because she planned to use a few feminine wiles if she had to. She didn't feel great about that part of it. Not that her boss had required her to use said wiles; Bud knew nothing about it. He assumed she was going on a regular vacation. Mindy had told her mom she was going to visit a friend back home for the weekend. She'd only reveal her true motive for the trip if she was successful.

No, not if. *When*.

She was good at that, at burying what she really desired in service of what she needed. There was what you wanted, and there was what the world would allow you to have, and she had learned early on that a lot of things she *wanted* were not allowed. Or rather, were simply not worth the price. Because there was a price to everything, and Mindy knew what she was willing to pay.

She glanced in the rearview and flipped an errant strawberry tress back over her shoulder, flattening her lips to redistribute the gloss she'd applied sometime back around San Antonio. She reassured herself she was not the same girl who'd left Bolero after high school. It wasn't a question of highlights and a personal shopper, or even those hours spent with an image consultant who'd groomed a big-haired small-town cheerleader to succeed in the ruthlessly polished, male-dominated business climate of Dallas. No, it was a matter of confidence. Mindy knew she could do this job. She just needed the chance to prove it. Let the guys dominate in the setting where she needed them to; in all other venues, she would fight for her own place.

I can do this. I can do this.

A dead armadillo was splattered across the highway about a mile before the turnoff. It was the third one she'd seen this trip. She was ready for a change. A dead possum, maybe, or a snake. She didn't hope to see any live wildlife.

Then, confounding her expectations, a rabbit bounded from the roadside into the brush as her little car zipped past. She grudgingly acknowledged the bucolic loveliness of the Texas hill country, and the fact that the bunny fit right in. The whole picture was more charming than she remembered. It had been a dry March and it was already getting hot, but the landscape was still green, the trees lush and shady, the hillsides made more interesting by the occasional intrusion of rough limestone or granite. Some small part of her soul eased at the sight of all that rugged rock and verdancy, the things Dallas lacked so conspicuously. She scolded that part of herself for a weakling and reminded it that Dallas was home now. Big, shiny, rich Dallas, where everybody called her Melinda.

Hilltop Ranch rode the border between the scenic hill country and the less appealing scrubland of West Texas. Mindy hoped most of the ranch was situated on the scenic side of that divide. She also hoped Logan Hill was stunned when she swept into view, the former homecoming queen returning like a diplomat on a state visit. An ambassador from the big city, the promised land of anywhere-but-Bolero. They would talk about old times, good times, and she would pretend to miss the rustic small town with its charming country ways.

Not that Logan knew her well enough to share many specific memories. He'd tutored her in math a few times when she was still in middle school, but she hadn't seen much of him in high school. Mindy had to consult her yearbook to recall that he'd been two years ahead of her. While she'd been swishing pompons and dating football players, Logan had spent his time with the Future Farmers of America, the marching band, and something called the Slide Rule Club—an apparent reference to the days before calculators, when math had actually involved a slide rule. She mostly remembered him as a long, gawky beanpole of a guy, nerdy in braces, with a crewcut that made his ears look like they stuck out. She had no idea what had become of him after he'd graduated. If he was still in Bolero, probably not that much.

But still, she could play this part, reminisce with Hill until he fell into a state of suggestibility. She could charm anyone. Schmoozing was a skill she'd spent a lot of time honing over the past few years, and not just at work. Her experiences in the Dallas kink scene had only made her better at it; learning to intrigue potential Doms, turn down unpalatable offers, and negotiate scenes beat the hell out of any of her business school classes when it came to giving her practical schmoozing experience. And in her fantasy—in which Logan sometimes remained his tall but scrawny seventeen-year-old self, braces and all, and at other times was a sadly paunchy aging hick—she saw herself winning over the man and sealing the deal with a single well-aimed smile. She wasn't the eager-to-please cheerleader anymore, but a woman of the world, sophisticated and—

"*In one hundred yards, turn left on—*"

"Oh, shut *up.*"

Mindy fumbled for her phone, turning off the annoying nasal voice of the GPS app before tossing the device back into the passenger seat. She didn't know why she'd used it anyway. She didn't need any navigation assistance for this trip. This was territory she'd conquered long ago, and left behind for better things. She hadn't been back in a dozen years, not since that summer after she graduated, but nothing had changed much. The familiarity was disconcerting. When she'd passed the City Limits sign, she'd had to swallow back a pang of something suspiciously like homesickness.

I can do this.

She turned when she reached Bolero, barely skimming the edge of town before heading back out of it. Instead of driving toward her childhood home, she veered deeper into the countryside, toward the future she was determined to make for herself.

Chapter Two

Mindy had never actually been to Hilltop Ranch before, though she must have driven past the main gate a thousand times or more growing up. She'd overestimated how long the drive would take by a good half hour or more. There was surprisingly little traffic coming out of Dallas–Fort Worth, probably because she'd escaped the metroplex area so early in the day. She'd even managed to hit San Antonio's outskirts at that golden lull between lunch and Friday afternoon rush hour. It was just a quarter past three when she turned from the county road onto the patchy asphalt of the ranch driveway. Another five minutes of slow meandering across the property, following faded signs around one hill and up another, finally brought her to the main parking lot, where she saw only a handful of trucks.

The place looked deserted, and when Mindy got out of her car she could hear nothing but birdsong and the distant sound of running water. She hoisted her suitcase and trekked along the gravel path that led from the parking area, following the arrows that pointed toward the main house. Along the way she caught glimpses of two of the guest cottages, but no people. No more vehicles. Nothing. She'd forgotten that about the country, how the silence could become so noticeable it was like a presence. It was almost eerie, even in the bright light of day. She welcomed the noisy *crunch* of her own footsteps on the walkway.

The temperature was already past warm and edging into hot, and things were starting to look parched; as usual, Texas needed rain. But she was encouraged by the sight and sound of a busy creek, which indicated they weren't quite at drought conditions yet. And when she rounded another bend in the path, veering away from the cheerful burbling, Mindy came across yet another vision of running water over rock-hard surfaces.

This one stopped her in her tracks.

I'd like one of those.

Well, who wouldn't? He was magnificent, a cowgirl's dream of a man, with a sleekly muscled back and broad shoulders. Not an ounce of fat that she could see, but he was certainly rounding out the seat of his jeans in a delicious way that made her want to grab on. The water-spotted, well-worn Wranglers molded to his ass and thighs like they were happy to have the job.

Water dripped down from the thick head of dark blond hair he'd slicked away from his face before putting his hat back on. She was just close enough to see how the rivulets outlined each defined muscle as they trickled down his back and sides, drawing the eye to those pleasing shapes, catching the afternoon sun and twinkling playfully along his gorgeous abs as he turned to face her.

Oh shit! She'd been caught blatantly ogling him. She could only hope he was flattered, not offended.

"Well, hey there," said Adonis in denim.

Mindy waved weakly with one hand, dropping her eyes from the man's six-pack in an automatically submissive gesture more suited for the club than for a business setting. "Hey. I'm one of the guests. I guess I'm a little early." She composed herself enough to drag her gaze back up to his face, where it belonged—and her jaw dropped.

No. Fucking. Way.

The man coming toward her, mopping off his phenomenal chest with a plaid shirt, was Logan Hill. He flashed a movie star-caliber grin at her as he approached, tipping his hat like a gentleman. No braces, no gawkiness. All grown up and then some. And then a little more on top of that. But recognizable, all the same.

"My God. Mindy Valek. I saw the name on the reservation, but I never put Melinda Valek together with Mindy from back in school. That last name is so common around here. How the hell are you? Wow!" Then he said the thing she least expected and least wanted to hear. "You haven't changed one bit."

Logan knew he needed to charm everybody, to wow the "crowd" of eight visitors. He prided himself on good presentation skills. But even as he launched into the welcoming spiel he'd worked up, he couldn't help sneaking glances at one guest in particular.

Mindy Valek. He hadn't been kidding when he'd said she hadn't changed a bit since high school. Still the same thick strawberry-blond hair. It was a little darker, she wore it a bit shorter now, and he figured she probably had a more complicated and expensive haircut, but the general impression hadn't changed. Same adorable freckles across the bridge of her nose, wide hazel eyes that that had always caught his attention because they always seemed to be smiling. Most importantly, the same knockout body that looked every bit as good as it had back in high school. She'd always seemed like the girl next door, if the girl next door had happened to be a ridiculously hot underwear model. And that *ass*. Her cheerleading uniform had just been the icing on the cake, although the snug T-shirt she currently wore was definitely an acceptable alternative.

Do not stare at the boobs of paying customers, some deep instinct prompted, and Logan snatched his gaze back to the group at large. Most of them were paying attention, either to Logan or to Charley, who waited patiently next to him, the cowboy's obligatory trusty steed. Logan took a gulp from the water bottle he held, and hoped his momentary distraction would be put down to a dry throat.

"You'll find a menu in your cabin, along with the schedule. Also a map with some of the restaurants in town, for lunch. Or you can let Robert know at breakfast if you'd like a box lunch, and he'll be happy to take care of that for you. I believe he even has a form you can fill out with choices and prices. If you decide to head out for dinner, just give Robert or me a heads-up so he doesn't cook too much. He told me to make sure I mentioned that," Logan said with a sheepish grin, "or else he'd come after me with the big skillet."

The little group chuckled, obviously a fairly easy crowd, and Logan relaxed as he continued. "I know some of you plan to do a little riding this week, and Lamar over there will be the go-to person for that. I can't offer you Charley here, but we have a number of fine riding horses and tomorrow morning Lamar will make sure you get matched up with the right mount and get whatever instruction you might need. He knows more about horses than most of us will ever forget. Isn't that right, Charley? Isn't it?"

On cue, the gray nodded his long head, to the audience's delight.

"Smartest hand on the ranch," Logan deadpanned, jerking a thumb toward the horse. "Also in your cabins is a map of the property. We don't want anybody lost, and we definitely want to keep the hunting confined to the designated areas. Which brings us to Diego. Wave hello to the folks, Diego." He looked expectantly over to his crew of three, perched in a row on the high rail fence of the paddock behind him. Diego waved, then doffed his straw hat with an extravagant flourish.

"Diego is our gamekeeper, and supervises all the hunting activity. Please make sure you talk to him this evening about the guidelines if you're planning to hunt, and also if you'd like to shoot trap or get in some target practice. And I guess that's pretty much it for now." Logan shifted the water bottle to his right hand, giving it a subtle *crinkle* and suppressing a grin when Charley took it with a snort and flutter of his velvety mouth. "Hey!"

The horse tipped his head back, swigging the last inch or so of water, and the guests and hands alike cracked up as Logan threw his battered Stetson down to the ground in a mock rage.

"Darn it, Charley, we've talked about this!"

Charley lowered his head, and Logan could practically see his eyes twinkling as he released the water bottle to his owner's waiting hand . . . then ducked down to grab the hat.

Logan glared, crossed his arms, and tapped his foot as the on-lookers cackled. Charley tossed his head in horsey glee, then obediently placed the crumpled hat back on Logan's head.

"I'll deal with you later," he promised the horse, then pasted on a long-suffering look as he turned back to the audience. "I hope you all have a wonderful week. Welcome to Hilltop Ranch!"

The happy group dispersed slowly, the two older couples chatting slowly as they walked toward the main path back to the cabins. The three men who'd come primarily to hunt wandered over to consult with Diego. Mindy was left alone, looking amused. She had her weight shifted to one foot, her thumbs hooked around her belt loops, a study in nonchalance. The late sun made a ridiculously bright halo of her hair.

Perhaps he'd wowed her after all. Stunned her into speechlessness with his brilliant comedic performance. Acting—yet another skill he hadn't realized he'd need in order to take over the family business.

"Charley Horse?" Mindy cocked her head. "Really?"

Not speechless, apparently.

"I didn't name him myself," Logan defended, as he patted the animal in question and fed him a hunk of carrot.

"Did you steal him from a circus or something?" Mindy came forward and let Charley snuffle her hand, then reached up to scratch behind one of his expressive ears.

Logan shook his head. "More like rescued him. My brother, Ethan, did, actually. You remember Ethan, right? I think he graduated the same year as you. He's a large animal vet now. Charley was in a traveling carnival, and one of the handlers called Ethan out to stitch up a cut on a different horse. He saw Charley there in the next stall, with one of the worst cases of navicular syndrome he'd ever seen. They were actually getting ready to ask Ethan what he'd charge to put the poor critter down, because his hooves just couldn't take all the hard surfaces and riding in the trailer anymore. He was lame all the time, and hurting. So Ethan called me, I staked him some cash, and we sprang Charley from that joint."

"Wow. He looks great now."

"It took us a good year to get his hooves back in shape and get the inflammation under control. But now it's all soft pastures and trails, and gentle physical therapy rides."

"And entertaining the customers."

"That, too," Logan agreed. "He seems to enjoy it. I think he missed performing during his hiatus."

"Well, who can blame him? He's a born showman, obviously. Lucky you had this place here to keep him."

Logan chuckled. "Well, he seems to be getting used to it. But no, for most of that time he was outside Houston, where I lived until a few months ago. Not too much work for engineers in Bolero."

"Oh. You . . . got out? I guess I just assumed—"

"I never left? No, I couldn't wait to leave. Four years at UT, then I went to work in Houston, bought a house there and everything. And I was probably a fool to come back. They say you can never go home again, but . . . well, here I am."

"Huh. Yeah, here we both are."

She propped one foot on the lowest fence rail, drawing Logan's eyes down to her legs and the skillfully distressed jeans that hugged her curves like a glove. He wished she was facing away from him—

it hadn't escaped his attention that her ass had somehow only grown more shapely and spankable since high school.

Do not think about spanking the asses of paying customers, either.

"So . . . now that I'm not sopping wet, showing people to cabins or helping Charley entertain the customers, I finally have time to ask. What brings *you* back to town, Mindy? I wouldn't have figured you for a dude ranch kinda girl."

Mindy leaned into the fence and hooked her boot heel more firmly over the bottom rail. How to answer?

The right answer, the only true answer, was that his ranch was sitting on a figurative gold mine, and she wanted to exploit that fact to further her own career. To put the land to its best use, according to the tenets of the oil and gas industry. To make them all money. "*Drill, baby, drill*" and all that. Time to get things out on the table.

But Logan was smiling at her, a real knee-melter of a smile. He was sticking around to make conversation as if he didn't have a million other things to do—but not like he was fawning over a popular girl, hoping to catch her eye. Like a friend. A very calm, in-charge kind of friend. It was throwing her off.

He was an engineer. And he did a comedy routine with his horse.

She didn't want the moment to end. She liked life so much better when she could please all of the people, all of the time. So she opened her mouth to tell one set of truths, but another came out.

"Nostalgia, I guess. I spent so much time helping Lamar out down at the stables growing up. I even used to lead trail rides for him. I wanted to spend some time riding again, and you'd just announced the grand reopening, so I figured, where better to spend my vacation?"

"That makes sense. Well, I appreciate it, anyway."

Guilt trickled a slimy path through Mindy's glow. She smiled weakly, eyes still on the horse. "Anything I can do to help." *As it please you, sir.* She longed, for a moment, to be in the club, or at a play party with a trusted Dom, somewhere she knew exactly what would happen if she did or didn't follow the rules. Where she knew what the rules *were*.

"Anything? You wouldn't happen to know anything about marketing, would you?" Logan joked.

"Nope, sorry. Why, do you need more publicity?"

"As much as I can get for a budget of . . . well, a very small budget, let's put it that way. I sank most of my liquid assets into buying this place and getting it up to code for guests."

So money's tight. He needs an angel. There's your opening, Mindy. You know how he can make enough money to buy space on every billboard in the state.

"I'm headed to the barn," Logan said before Mindy could frame her offer. "I need to put Charley up. Hey, it's still early. You should come with me and get Lamar to hook you up with a mount. Avoid the rush later."

"Oh . . . sure, okay."

Whatever Mindy had planned to say was lost in the jumble of guilt, lust, and other thoughts that spilled through her brain as Logan hiked his foot up to the stirrup and swung his leg over the saddle. It was all just a whirl of squeaking leather and denim stretched taut over powerful thighs. When the hell had he filled out like that?

Logan was holding out his hand, looking down at her like it didn't occur to him she'd decline to take it. "Hop on. It'll be faster."

She did it almost automatically, toe finding the stirrup he'd momentarily vacated, arm flexing against the pull of their clasped hands for leverage as she lifted off. There was an awkward moment as she shifted into position against the back of the saddle, when she grabbed for leather and may or may not have accidentally groped a certain amount of denim-clad cowboy butt along the way. Then she had to figure out where to put her hands, finally settling them on Logan's waist as Charley started the short stroll to the barn.

Lamar assessed Mindy's skills as rusty but adequate, and matched her to a slightly standoffish but soft-mouthed bay mare with a gait like flowing water. Mindy hadn't been on horseback since leaving Bolero, but she found that after a few minutes, it all started coming back to her. Even out of practice, she could tell when she was riding a quality animal.

"This is no rescue horse," she called to Logan, who watched from Charley's back as Mindy put the mare through her paces.

"You're right about that. Poppy is my mom's horse, actually. I'm not supposed to let the customers ride her, but she needs the exercise. And you're sort of similar to an old friend, so I think I can get away with it. You used to ride dressage, right?"

A lifetime ago, all through elementary and into middle school. She had stopped competing when she started cheerleading in high school, because there just wasn't enough time in the day. When her family moved to Dallas, they'd taken their horses, but her dad had kept them in the divorce he'd initiated a few months later.

"It's been a while," she admitted.

"You've still got a great seat."

His smile was too slow and broad to be anything but suggestive. He was confident in a way that bordered on arrogance, and *ping*ed her unique sexual radar loud and clear. He certainly hadn't ever smiled like *that* back in high school. Although maybe he had, and the braces just spoiled the effect. It was disconcerting, seeing the boy she'd known as this almost too-handsome, too-confident man. She'd recognized him easily enough, some essence of him hadn't changed . . . but at the same time, *everything* had changed. Mindy didn't like to think of herself as shallow, so she stuffed down the flashback of water caressing Logan's sun-kissed chest, the association of him with the smell of warm leather tack, and concentrated instead on the animal beneath her. The little bay mare felt tense, fractious after going too long without a rider. She would take some watching, and Mindy was out of practice. Extra caution would be required.

She swept past Logan and Charley at a slow, controlled canter, and caught his appreciative nod from the corner of her eye. He looked like a good guy in a Western, white horse and all, like the Lone Ranger without the mask to hide his beauty. But that smile was pure Black Bart. Mindy had been foolish and conceited to assume she could wrap him around her finger; she'd be lucky to keep herself from acting like a fool over the man Logan Hill had become.

Extra caution would *definitely* be required.

Chapter Three

Logan excused himself after only a few minutes of watching her ride, and Mindy tried not to make a spectacle of herself watching him ride away. Watching his horse's ass, to be specific, since Logan himself never looked back. She wouldn't admit to herself that she was watching Logan's ass. She knew herself well enough to know that nothing good ever came from ogling the asses of vanilla men. That way lay only disappointment and bitterness on both sides.

But *damn*. He not only looked like Fantasy Cowboy Dom, he literally smelled like horse, leather, and yes, *man*. If e-books could be worn out through overuse, by now Mindy would have run through several copies of a few cherished romance novels featuring heroes who were more or less Logan Hill captured on the page.

Except for the financial insecurity and the goofy horse, she reminded herself. A romance novel Dom would be a billionaire oil mogul who ranched as a sideline—J. R. Ewing with a bullwhip. Or some younger, more picturesque version of her stepfather. Never mind that the actual Doms of Mindy's acquaintance tended to be network analysts, or mid-management types. Or engineers. Fantasies were fantasies for a reason.

"'Bout time to call it a night, here," suggested Lamar from his perch on the paddock rail. "It'll be supper time soon."

He hopped down, and Mindy let Poppy have her head to trot in his direction. The mare stopped neatly one pace away from him, making no fuss during dismount. She seemed to have calmed down a bit during the course of even that short ride, and she really was a pleasure to work with; Mindy couldn't wait to see how she did on the trail.

"So, how have you been, Lamar? You're not going to tell me I look just the same, too, are you?"

"Logan said that? *Pfft*. Boy's an idiot. They ain't feeding you in Dallas, I guess," the old man chided as he walked the mare back to her stall.

"I just don't have time to eat." It was the airy stock response she always gave. Everyone said it, nobody meant it. In her world, the statement was code for *I count every calorie, and spend an hour a day at the gym or in spin class. I have nightmares about hidden carbohydrates. I would kill somebody for a truly guilt-free piece of chocolate cake.*

"That's a shame." In Lamar's world, apparently it just meant you didn't have time to eat. "You'll eat good here, Robert knows what he's doing in the kitchen. And you'll have time. Enough to do some riding, too. I can see you're rusty."

"I haven't been on a horse since the summer before I left for college. I'm lucky I didn't just fall right off," she joked.

She was also rusty with the tack, apologizing to Lamar and Poppy several times in the course of unsaddling as she flipped straps the wrong way and dropped things everywhere. What had once been second nature now felt as awkward as toddling. By the time she slipped the reins back on their hook in the tack room, she felt curiously exhausted.

Lamar was quick to reassure her. "You'll pick it back up. By the end of the week you'll be helping me give the lessons again."

Mindy laughed, recalling all the times she'd helped Lamar and his wife at their boarding stables near her home, giving lessons to younger kids in between training sessions. She'd ridden Western and English dressage back then, back before high school. Before cheerleading and unexpected popularity had siphoned away her free time, and her parents began to push so hard to move away from Bolero. At one point in seventh grade or so, she was sure she and her horse, Jimbo, were destined for international competition, with Lamar as her coach all the way. That seemed like another life entirely now. She'd heard her father had sold Jimbo to some family with a little girl.

"You and Margaret still have the stables?"

The old man tugged at his beard. "Naw, we sold out a couple

years ago. Bewliss owns it now. Along with about half the property on Jackson Street. But his daughter, Jane, is doing a good job running it, and she has some good folks giving the lessons. Not too bad."

"Mr. Bewliss . . . he isn't still the mayor, is he?"

"Who else? Nobody but him wants the job."

"Jeez. Things really are just the same."

"They get more the same every year," Lamar agreed with a snort. "Maybe you should head into town some time this week, see for yourself."

Mindy shrugged, noncommittal. She might drive into town—some time when she wasn't trying to talk herself into doing the job she'd come here for. "We'll see."

"You're wasting your time, you know."

She was startled enough to stop in her tracks for a second. Lamar kept on walking, and she trotted after him. "I beg your pardon?"

"You heard me, missy. Logan may not know who the Valek girl ended up going to work for, but I sure do. It's a small town, and your daddy's people are still from here, even if your daddy moved away and left you and your momma high and dry. We still get the gossip. I'm happy to see you again, but if that's your plan for the whole week—nagging my boss about a mineral lease—then you might as well grab your bags and head on out right now, 'cause it ain't happenin'. Ain't nobody gonna talk Logan into selling away them rights." His tone was sympathetic, even if his words were harsh.

"It's not nagging. It's negotiation, and it's what I do for a living." It was at least what she hoped to do for a living, even if she wasn't quite there yet. And damn the tiny town grapevine. "And a lease isn't a sale." This was technically true—although in Texas, once those rights were leased away and oil exploration started, they were nearly always gone for good in practice. Especially if the exploration was successful.

Lamar shot her a look full of subtext she didn't want to read. "Suit yourself, then. Guess you've changed, after all. Have a good night, Miss Mindy." It was clearly a dismissal.

"Oh. Well, you, too, Lamar." After another few steps, she stopped and let him go on without her.

He was clear of the stable yard before she allowed herself to acknowledge what was about to happen. He was going to tell Logan. She'd missed her window. Now Logan would be suspicious of her motives—rightly so—and she'd never even get the chance to sell him on the benefits of a deal. She'd lost, because she hadn't even realized the game had started long before she stepped foot on the ranch.

Should she have tried to deny it? Claimed that the reasons she'd given Logan for her stay here—which were, after all, *completely true*—were the *complete truth*?

And not only had she screwed up, but she'd gambled a sizable chunk of her savings to pay for this now-pointless "vacation." Almost a month's rent, or a few months' worth of car payments. If she lost the job, though, that month or so of extra cushion really wouldn't help her much anyway. Or so she tried to tell herself, since she was stuck here now either way.

Fuck. Stuck, and kind of lost. She should have gotten directions from Lamar. Now she wasn't even sure which way her cabin was.

Trying to get her bearings, she turned in a slow half circle, taking in the distant barn and stable buildings, the wide lawn and scattered trees in front of the main house . . . and yes, the head of the gravel path that led down the hillside and off toward the guest cabins. Everything was lit in shades of rose gold, as the sun melted into the hilltops. The breeze carried a hint of something sweet and spicy, magnolia maybe, and the soft churring symphony of the evening creatures was tuning up. Despite those noises, it was quiet, so quiet—a deep-in-the-bone stillness that Dallas could never offer her.

Mindy shook her head and cast off the spell of the sunset. She made herself move, setting out for her cabin to get a flashlight before she returned to the main house for dinner. Her practical, analytical mind told her she was too young to be sentimental, and reminded her that even if she lost her job, she'd find another one in Dallas because it was the land of opportunity. Bolero, conversely, was the armpit of Texas, and she'd been thrilled to get out.

Her senses, meanwhile, rejoiced in coming home.

Logan wanted to punch something.

Jameson. He wanted to punch Bud fucking Jameson, for spoiling his mood and sending his luscious lackey to spy. If it hadn't been for Jameson, Logan wouldn't have seen Mindy Valek again, wouldn't have thought there was a spark there, wouldn't have made an idiot of himself staring at her like a lovestruck schoolboy.

Wouldn't have entertained the notion that she might be staring back. Wouldn't have ever *seen* her ass, much less gotten fixated on the idea of taking his hand—or a paddle, or maybe even a bullwhip—to it.

What the hell was he thinking? He should have suspected something was up from the first moment he recognized her. A girl like that didn't come to a dude ranch for a vacation, especially not alone. Former homecoming queens came back to town in state, guest-starring at people's baby showers and holding court at class reunions. They didn't need to sneak into the outskirts of town and hide out on a guest ranch, riding horses and shooting guns for a week. There were horses and shooting ranges in Dallas, if Mindy really wanted to do those things.

Of course, there had been horses and ranges in Houston, too, but here Logan was. Almost out of money, certainly out of his depth. But strangely enjoying himself despite the tension. He wanted the ranch to work out, and today he'd actually felt for a time like it might after all. He'd liked meeting the guests, making them comfortable. He was looking forward to the week, getting to know these folks and helping them find things to do with their time at the ranch. He'd been nervous, but it felt right all the same, greeting the little crowd and giving them the rundown. Orchestrating things. It had been fun.

Until Lamar had broken the news that Mindy Valek was an agent of the devil.

Logan didn't know why she'd bothered to lie about it, to pretend she was here for a vacation. The more he thought about it, the angrier he got at that part. Jameson had obviously gotten tired of the runaround on the phone and sent somebody to confront Logan in person. Somebody who seemed ideal for sweet-talking Logan into this scheme. What would she have told her boss? That Logan Hill was the dweeb who used to tutor her in math? That she could have him eating out of the palm of her hand?

The cynic in him wondered how far she'd intended to go to secure the deal. Flirting? Seduction? Maybe he should milk the situation a little before flat-out telling her it was a waste of her time. He'd come into his own now, figured his shit out, and he was no slouch at mind games; he could have had little Mindy eating out of the palm of *his* hand if he'd wanted to, even without the overtly kinky stuff that would no doubt horrify her.

"Who am I kidding?" Logan mumbled, jerking the refrigerator door open and extracting a frosty longneck. People didn't do that sort of thing. *He* didn't do that sort of thing. The cynic in him existed, but it was a puny thing, easily overwhelmed by the manners and values instilled in him since birth. Besides, he was a Dom, not a pickup artist. Mindy might be a manipulative liar, but that didn't mean she was a tramp bent on sleeping her way into business deals. And even if she was intent on that, it didn't mean Logan was ever going to take advantage of it. Of her.

Even if it had been a while. Far too long, in fact. Months. *Jesus.*

He took a long pull off his beer and thought about Allison, his ex-girlfriend, currently on a cruise in the Bahamas with the guy she'd started seeing after she left Logan. She'd thought the whole guest-ranch scheme was insane, and she'd told him so. The lack of support had come at the worst possible time; their breakup after that conversation would have been inevitable even if she hadn't been stuck in Houston for her job. Not that he'd asked her to come to Bolero with him; he'd never even considered that. But he would have been fine with a long-distance relationship. Except it wouldn't have lasted long, anyway, because he and Allison were already nearly at the end. Knowing that didn't make the end any easier, though. She hadn't just scoffed at the plan, she'd scoffed at Logan, calling him a loser and an idiot.

Logan realized soon after she left that Allison had always been kind of a bitch, and that she'd been unpleasantly inclined to top from the bottom. Not that she'd necessarily been wrong about the relative sanity of the scheme to start the ranch back up. And she'd almost certainly been right to assess his use of his life savings for this purpose as less than wise. But she'd been, to his mind, needlessly blunt in her response. He'd seen that quality in her before, but it was different being on the receiving end of it in a non-sexual context.

Allison would definitely call him some choice names for refusing to even discuss a mineral lease with Bud Jameson. It was money on the table, there for the taking, and all he had to do was sign away some rights to parts of his land he never saw anyway. Except that he would see it being wrecked when the oil company inevitably used those "sub-surface" rights to destroy the land in their quest to get at the black gold underneath. He knew *exactly* what the land was worth, and what would happen to it . . . though he was glad Mindy had no idea just how well he knew. Glad he hadn't told her what *kind* of engineer he was: a petroleum engineer. God only knew who Jameson would've sent in her place if she'd reported back *that* little tidbit.

Logan knew what drilling would do to the place, because he'd been around it all his professional life. Fracking would be even worse, if they went that route. He didn't want that to happen to *his own land*. Even so, from a partial lease the money could help keep him afloat awhile longer. He'd given a lot of thought to leasing.

Not to Jameson, though, who'd taken an all-or-nothing approach to every offer he'd made Logan, and who'd made it clear he would keep hammering away until Logan cracked. And he wouldn't lease to anybody who worked for Jameson, no matter how perky her boobs were, no matter how rounded her ass. No matter how bright a toothpaste-commercial smile she flashed his way. No matter how sweetly she wrapped her plush, curvy lips around his—

"'Bout ready for dinner, sir?"

Robert's entrance broke Logan's train of thought and deflated his unfortunate response to the unexpectedly vivid image he'd been conjuring.

"Sure, let's get it set out. And remember, cool it with the 'sir.' This isn't the club or a leather household. 'Boss' will do just fine."

Robert grinned and fluttered his startlingly long lashes. "I'll do my best . . . boss. But old habits, and all that."

"Consider it an order."

"Ooh, hot. I always did yearn for you to give me orders, s— boss."

Robert knew he wasn't Logan's type, but Logan didn't mind the teasing. His Domly ego enjoyed a little unrequited adulation now and then, regardless of the source. If only Robert's demure eyelash-flickering didn't recall an almost identical look from a certain strawberry-haired princess earlier.

Logan grimaced and adjusted his jeans once the cook's back was turned. He couldn't seem to help himself where Mindy Valek was concerned. Even after all these years, just thinking about her still gave him an almost instant boner. It had been horrific in high school, the stealthy dance of arousal and secrecy he and so many other guys played in the halls and under their desks, particularly on game days when the cheerleaders wore their uniforms to class. Oh, the lurid classroom-set spanking fantasies of his high school days! He had more control now, but not nearly as much as he'd thought.

Logan helped lay out the settings on the long farmhouse table that had been in the dining room since the early days of his grandparents' marriage. The guests started to arrive, and he put his raconteur smile back on for the duration. Each *flap* and *clap* of the front screen door opening and closing drew Logan's eyes to the end of the dining room. When he realized he was waiting for Mindy to arrive, he forced her out of his mind and focused on the business at hand. He had a whole week to address that *other* business. And address it he most certainly would.

Chapter Four

She hadn't anticipated a roommate.

Apparently the spider hadn't anticipated Mindy, either. It had retreated to the corner of its enormous web when Mindy breezed into the cabin, and now they were simply staring at each other, each waiting for the other to make the first move.

Or at least Mindy thought the spider was staring at her. It was hard to tell with spiders. Even one as big as this one.

It was an orb weaver, she knew that much. Its web spanned one corner of the bedroom ceiling in an elegant sweep, looking for all the world like a Halloween decoration. The spider looked like one, too. It was nearly as big as her hand, with striking black markings on its leg joints. There were already a few mosquitos trapped in the web.

"Where's a broom when you need one? Or a vacuum cleaner?"

The spider didn't answer. Mindy pulled out her phone and found just enough signal to search the internet. Yes, it was an orb weaver. No, it wasn't likely to bite her. It would probably just stay in its web over in the far corner, gorging itself on mosquitos, which would then not have the opportunity to suck her blood.

"Okay," she conceded. "You can stay. But only because I don't have a good way to kill you without you falling down on my head. And only because you didn't build the damn web right over the bed. Smart spider."

Aside from the unexpected additional occupant, the cabin was nicer than she'd expected. Rustic log walls appeared worse for the wear outside, but were smoothed and nicely weatherproofed inside. It wasn't quite hot enough yet to make the window unit air conditioner a necessity, but at least there was one. The mattress on the queen-size bed was nicely made, the bed linens fine hotel quality. All the rough-hewn log furniture was meticulously cleaned and dusted, and the few accent pieces in the room were charming. A vase from a local pottery, a pair of watercolors of San Antonio landmarks. Even the towels in the tiny bathroom were thick and soft, and there was a basket of toiletries on the counter, also from local companies.

All in all, it seemed like a lovely place to spend a week of vacation. In other circumstances she thought she'd really enjoy it. She unpacked her things, laid her cosmetics out in the bathroom, and reminded herself that the trip was an investment in her future career.

She'd intended to head for the main house for dinner after she'd unpacked, but once outside the cabin, her feet took her back to the stable. A few solar lights were staked around, and she hoped they'd be enough to help her navigate back to the cabin once full dark fell. She was hungry after the afternoon's exercise, the long drive—the general stress of the day. For the moment, though, she was more in need of another taste of the stable's comfort: the familiar, hazy smell of horse and hay and . . . home.

Poppy accepted the handful of sweet feed Mindy grabbed from a bin near the main door. The horse's long, elegant face was shadowed, nearly black in the gathering gloom. Mindy wondered if lights for the stable were on the to-do list, or if Logan planned to keep things as dark as possible. A break, for his guests, from the light pollution of Texas's cities and seemingly endless suburbs.

"Come for the horseback riding, stay for the view of the Milky Way," she murmured to Poppy. Her voice sounded harsh and out of place against the almost-disquieting stillness, and a prickling sensation ran up her spine, prompting her to glance over her shoulder in age-old instinct. Nobody was there. Just more horses, neatly stabled, innocently browsing for scraps in their feed bins.

It's quiet. Too quiet.

She thought about every horror movie she'd ever seen, and recognized that if she were in one of them, this would be the scene where the insane killer ambushed her in the barn with a pitchfork.

Across the aisle, one of the horses snorted and twitched at a fly, the stamp and swish filling the dead air in a comforting way. Mindy shook her head at her own foolishness, and proceeded into Poppy's stall with a curry comb. As she passed the bristles over the dark hair, Mindy mused on the power of guilt to mess with a person's mind.

Poppy seemed indifferent to the grooming, but it eased Mindy's mind to do the simple, repetitive task. When the horse grew more restive, Mindy gave her neck a final pat and slipped back out of the stall, moving down the row to the tack room, where she'd put up her saddle and bridle earlier under Lamar's watchful eye. The saddle had been as dusty as the horse, and she'd noticed at the time it could use a polish. Now she started poking around the supply shelf for some oil and a rag.

It was ridiculous for her to be there at all, more ridiculous still for her to be wasting time and energy on menial tasks that Logan probably already paid somebody to do. If she were thinking with her head instead of what was in her pants, she would be gone by now. No good could come of any further talks between her and Logan, not once he talked to Lamar. Although she'd be sure to apologize for not being honest with him from the start, the very next time she saw him.

The very next time—

"Mindy."

She jumped with a shriek, whirling to face the serial killer at the door, bracing for the pitchfork attack.

It was Logan. He didn't have a pitchfork, but Mindy wasn't completely reassured. Some instinct made her back up at the look on his face. Not scowling, not frowning, but she could still read anger there. Anger and more. She took another step back and found herself with nowhere left to go. Her back pressed firmly against the wall between the supply shelf and the bridle rack. She tried to look like she was just leaning there casually.

Fuck. Fuck fuck fuck fuck—

"You weren't hungry?"

It took her a second to process the question. She'd been expecting an accusation. But his voice was soft, cool. He stalked toward her, trailing his fingers along the neat row of bridles, toying with the reins.

"I wasn't in the mood for conversation. And actually I was just leaving. I wanted to head back to my cabin. It's getting a little chilly. Maybe time for a jacket."

"Yeah, there's a chill, all right." He stopped directly in front of her, still holding a rein from the closest bridle in one hand. "And I'm sure it's hard to chitchat when you're working on keeping your story straight."

The look in his eyes wasn't just anger, it was betrayal, and that could only mean one thing. "You had a chitchat with Lamar?"

Logan smiled, but not in a nice way. She tried to smile back but failed, because she felt too sick to manage. Eyeing the tack room door wistfully, she wondered whether she had a chance at making a break for it, literally running away from her problems. Getting into her car and disappearing into the night.

"An enlightening talk, one might say." He took one of her hands in his and, before she could protest, wrapped her wrist snugly with the end of the rein and tucked in the tail to secure the loops against her skin. The well-used leather tied well enough to hold her, and the bridle was on a high hook. She couldn't reach it, and couldn't jerk it down without damaging it. The disconnect between this setting and the one where she was usually tied up was beyond unsettling. Her heart pounded, and instead of the outrage she knew she ought to feel, she felt a delicious slide of arousal low in her belly.

"Hey. Um, okay. Wh—whatcha doing?"

Logan caught her other wrist up in a halter lead he'd snatched from one of the nearby hooks. It didn't hold quite as tight as the rein on the other side, but once he'd looped it around the shelf bracket by her shoulder, it did well enough. He'd roped and tied her as quickly and efficiently as an errant calf he needed to brand, albeit with leather and nylon instead of a lasso. His shirtsleeves were rolled back, revealing muscular forearms that flexed as he secured her. Mindy's mind, primed for kink, offered an image of Logan hog-tying her. *Not helpful.*

"You had a look in your eye like you were fixing to bolt. I'm just making sure you stay put," he explained, placing his hands on the wall just over her shoulders and leaning in until he was talking right next to her ear. "While we *chitchat.* Wouldn't want you running off to your cabin for a jacket, or suddenly remembering a work phone call you had to make, or anything like that. Lamar is up at the house helping Robert out with cleanup, and everybody else has headed back to their cabins. Gives us some nice, uninterrupted private time."

"Oh." Her voice was a tiny, pathetic thing, which was about right considering how she felt. Miserable, mortified . . . weirdly and inappropriately turned on by Logan's sudden shift from cowboy-next-door to dangerous outlaw. Every puff of his breath against her neck sent shivers down her spine. He could tie her to the railroad tracks and—*no, no, stop all that, Mindy, pull yourself together.*

"I'll untie you if you tell me to, because otherwise I'd be breaking the law. But somehow I don't think you'll tell me to. Now, I'm going to ask you one more time, one *last* time. What brings you here, Miss Valek?"

She exhaled with an unintended whimper. "A sincere desire to get back in touch with my roots?"

"You'll forgive me if I find that hard to believe."

He pulled back just far enough to stare directly at her, his glare uncompromising. Mindy wasn't physically intimidated. In fact, she was sure if she asked, he would untie her just as he'd said he would, and let her leave immediately. She was also sure if that happened, she would never see Logan again. That prospect already seemed unimaginable to her.

"I came here for work, because I knew my boss wanted your mineral rights. I was trying to prove myself to him. If I could bring back a deal, I'd have a shot at avoiding the next firing round, and maybe even doing some *real* work for the company."

"*Dammit!*" He thumped the wall by her head with both hands, then sagged toward her, shoulders slumped. His posture telegraphed his disappointment.

"And I'm really, really sorry I wasn't honest from the start," she added. She was sorry about a lot of things. Miserable, in fact.

"So am I."

"I had no right to come here and turn this week into one long hard sell. I was an idiot and a creep."

"Yes, you were."

Oh no. She was starting to cry. Big, fat tears, rolling down her face. She managed to wipe one eye then the other against her shoulders, then straightened to see Logan glaring at her with renewed fury.

"Cut that out."

Her mouth curled into a rueful twist, and her forehead started to ache. "I'm not doing it on purpose." It was something she'd had to train herself out of at work, something she usually only gave free rein to in the safety of a club or play party. And even then, only occasionally. The freedom to weep when challenged by authority figures. It was the impromptu bondage, she thought—crossing her signals, opening the floodgates during what should have been a purely business-like conversation.

"Jesus. You're manipulative to the bone, aren't you?"

"No," she insisted. "No! I'm not manipulative at all—that's the *problem*." The truth of this stunned her into a momentary silence. She mulled over the words as she snuffled back more tears. "I'm sorry, sir—um. Sorry, Logan."

"What was that?"

"Nothing. *God*."

Her wires were hopelessly crossed. She knew she ought to ask him to untie her—hell, or work her hands free on her own, she was pretty sure she could do that—and just *go*. But she couldn't make herself do it.

Logan folded his arms and scowled for a few seconds, then cursed and reached for the roll of rough brown paper towels on the supply shelf. He ripped a length off with unnecessary force and dabbed at Mindy's face, then held a dry portion to her nose.

"Blow," he ordered. After a moment, she complied. It didn't matter what Logan thought of her anymore anyway. Her humiliation was complete.

"Explain how you're not being manipulative." He tossed the wadded paper towel into the trash can in the corner, then refolded his arms and stared her down, his legs braced wide like he was ready for a fight. "You come here under false pretenses, planning to sucker me into some deal for your own benefit. You sweet-talk me, let me think you like me, for God's sake. Then when I call you out for lying to me, you start weeping like a hurt baby. How is any of that not an attempt to manipulate me?"

"I didn't mean any of it like that. It sounds awful when you say it, but it wasn't like that, Logan. I really *do* like it here. I—" The truth struck her the second before she said it. "I had pretty much given up on the deal. I was never gonna make it work anyway. And I *do* like you. I thought you liked me, and that was so great, and I hadn't expected any of that. I knew if I tried to bring the lease up, all that would go away, and the week would be a total loss. The flirting part just made it worse."

His scowl deepened. "I don't flirt. Wait, so you're saying my flirting was *bad*?"

"It was wonderful. But I hadn't planned on doing that. Or on . . . *meaning* it."

"Then why . . . what did you come here expecting, Mindy? If not this, then what did you think you were going to find?"

She shrugged, as best she could within the limitations of the re-straints, and felt embarrassed all over again. But she wouldn't com-pound her problems by adding more deceit to the mix. He deserved the truth. "Some pathetic, balding drugstore cowboy who'd spent his whole life in his hometown because he had to, not because he wanted to. Someone who never got out, and might be impressed by me pre-tending like I was something. And yes, I thought I might flirt a little if I needed to. But I would *never* have gone any further with it. Never."

"I would've."

"I would've, too, after seeing you." *Crap.* Being tied up was like a truth serum, apparently. She twisted her hands to grip the leather and nylon, the back of her mind noting with approval that he'd left her enough slack not to interfere with circulation. The man clearly knew how to tie a girl up. In other circumstances, she'd be thrilled by that knowledge. "But not to get the deal."

Logan pursed his lips, considering her. His gaze flicked over her hands, apparently checking the bonds as if it was automatic to do so. "So, just for the sake of argument, you would have let me, say . . . kiss you, if there was no land deal involved? If you'd just come here on vacation like you said?"

Her eyes were welling with tears again as she nodded. She looked down at the rough stones paving the floor, and watched a pair of drops fall to darken the dusty limestone. "I did come here on vaca-tion. I really did. I mean, I planned to try for the deal, I planned to be straightforward about it, but . . . I'm not sure what happened."

In her line of vision, Logan's boots stepped forward until he was toe to toe with her. Another teardrop spattered down, hitting dark leather this time. His chest brushed her forehead and she leaned there, wishing she could stay like that indefinitely. Mortified though she was, it was still comforting. He smelled so good. When he spoke, his voice sounded rumbly, vibrating against her skull.

"It was Mr. Clapsaddle, by the way. At the feed store."

"What?"

He hooked a finger under her chin and tipped her head up. She wasn't sure whether to be relieved or more worried to see a slightly cynical, cockeyed smile on his lips. "That's who told Lamar about you working for your stepfather. How Clapsaddle knew you were visiting here, I have no idea. It's that Bolero grapevine. Maybe your mom told somebody else's mom who has a cousin who sat next to Arlene Clapsaddle in church, who knows? I'm going to let you go in a minute, by the way."

"In a minute? Why not just let me go now, Logan? I'll clear out and leave you in peace. I know you're never going to deal with my stepfather's company." The idea of him letting her go was suddenly the worst part of all. She didn't want to leave. She didn't want him to release her. *All tied up* was her comfort zone, the only part of the current situation she absolutely knew what to do with.

He moved closer, his fingers still trapping her chin. The harsh edge was back in his expression. "That's probably true. But once I untie you, you'll be out the door, and I wasn't quite ready for you to go yet. I had one more point to make first."

"Oh?" Mindy's mind and heart were racing, her body responding to Logan's proximity while her head tried to sort out what he might mean.

She didn't have to puzzle over it for long. A moment later, his lips captured hers in a take-no-prisoners kiss. Her startled gasp was all the opportunity Logan needed to invade her mouth, but the moment she started to respond he drew back to tease his way over to her ear.

"I'm not too proud to admit if you *had* tried using sex as a bargaining tactic, we might be having a conversation about mineral leases right now. I still wouldn't have sold the rights, but it could've been an interesting chitchat."

Was that a suggestion? A threat? A compliment? Mindy cared for another two seconds, until Logan swiped his tongue over that spot behind her ear, the one that melted her knees and fried her brain. His hands roamed, exploring her in forays from her waist. First up, almost grazing the undersides of her breasts. Then down, curving behind her to cup her ass and pull her closer. He was so hard she almost felt bad for him. Whatever Logan was doing to her, he was clearly doing to himself, as well.

He kissed her again, channeling lust and anger into every possessive move of his tongue, into the rough grasp of his hands on her body.

When he pulled away without warning, she swayed forward, clutching the rein and halter lead for balance as Logan stepped back. Panting, he hesitated for a moment before blurting, "Well, I guess I showed you."

If she'd had even a single one of her wits about her, she probably would have laughed. But of all the things she was feeling as she leaned toward Logan, amusement wasn't among them. He untied her bonds with quick, jerky movements, not meeting her eyes.

Mindy hissed as she brought her arms down, wrapping them around her to stretch her shoulders. The muscles twitched from the strain, vibrating in a way that suggested they'd be sore tomorrow from the unaccustomed use. Pitiful. Her stamina wasn't what it used to be.

"I'm sorry," she offered again, since it seemed to apply on several levels at the moment. Sorry he'd stopped. Sorry he'd ever started. Sorry about his possible blue balls, and that she'd ever come to his ranch in the first place. She was a sorry, sorry specimen of a woman. "I'd better get going."

"No."

Stunned, she looked up at him. "No?"

Logan looked embarrassed. "I mean, you're free to go if you want. But damned if I'll refund your money. So you might as well stay the week."

"Because I'm a paying customer."

He nodded. "Ma'am."

She coughed into her hand, looking toward the door. Logan stepped out of her way, and she moved in that direction but turned with her hand on the doorknob, considering a handshake. A second later, she thought better of it. Best not to touch him. In fact, that was probably the only way.

She nodded back at him, then opened the door and headed out into the night.

Chapter Five

Crocodile tears.

Had to be. Logan chided himself for ten kinds of fool as he strode through the cooling night air, making a final round to check that all was well before he turned in.

He also wanted to give himself time for full boner deflation before he went back to the house. Robert was never one to let a hard dick go by without a comment. And detecting them was one of his superpowers.

It wasn't easy, though. Logan kept thinking of the scene in the barn, and then there the damn thing would go again. Because it had felt like a *scene*, hadn't it, and he'd craved nothing more than to get Mindy naked and start leaving marks until, when she cried, he knew for certain the tears were real.

He had lost his head at one point in there, he knew that much. Maybe when she'd bowed her head like that, standing so still and penitent, but graceful and proud at the same time. So like a remorseful submissive, it had seemed the most natural thing in the world to restrain her in some way. To keep her from rattling apart until he could decide what to do with her. And then . . . it had seemed to have exactly that effect on her, holding her together. And after he'd lashed the first wrist to the shelf, she'd offered up her other hand without his even having to ask . . . seemingly without realizing she'd done it.

And then she'd relaxed into the bonds and said the thing he couldn't get off the auto-play in his mind.

Sir. Why did it have to be "*sir*"? And he wouldn't have thought twice about it—this was Texas, people still said "sir" and "ma'am"—except that she'd caught herself and changed it as if she'd said something wrong.

His cock thrummed against his fly, complaining silently about the neglect. *Patience, Sparky.*

As he walked down the path past the cabins, he dragged his thoughts back to the substance of the conversation. The mineral rights. Bud fucking Jameson. And Mindy, Bud's paid lackey. They wanted the use of what lay under Logans land? They'd get it over his dead body. He came from a long line of holdouts, and the ranch's position on the underlying granite substrate had even foiled previous attempts at sneaky, underhanded slant-well drilling from neighboring properties. The bulk of the land was basically in the middle of a natural underground moat. If there was oil, nobody was getting it without going straight through Logan Hill—and that was not happening.

His palm itched, and he slapped it against his thigh, the sound falling curiously flat in the thick evening air. This part of the trail was bounded by shrubbery, deadening noise as it provided privacy. All the cabins still had some lights on. Everything seemed to be in order.

That palm wanted something softer than his own leg to land against. His own hand conspired with his brain to remind him of Mindy's butt, and how tempting it had felt during the brief, mad grope he'd allowed himself.

Jesus. She'd been so pliant in his grip, whimpering and fucking melting against him when he stole that kiss. As if she were already turned on, already getting into the scene, maybe aroused by the bondage. Probably a rope bunny . . .

Oh.

He was so stunned he stopped in the path halfway between the cabins and the trailhead, then whirled to look back through the gloom at the warm glow from the window he knew was hers.

The way she'd offered her hand. The way her pupils had been blown the few times she'd lifted her gaze from the floor. The way she'd seemed to become more relaxed, not less, by the restraints and his manhandling.

Sir.

No. Nope. No way could he let himself think what he was thinking, not even for a second. Because it was just wishful, that was all, wishful thinking he had no call to be doing about Treacherous Mindy. No. The high school cheerleader crush-from-afar did not walk back into your life a decade later and turn out to be a kinkster.

Much less a submissive. Bottom to his top. Yin to his kinky yang. Impossible.

And even if she were, which she was not, it wouldn't matter. Because treachery.

His right hand ached, and he realized he'd been clenching it into a fist. He forced the fingers to relax and turned resolutely back toward the main house. With every step away from her cabin, though, he felt a stronger and stronger pull to turn around.

Allison had been about compromise; she'd fit so neatly into his day-to-day life in so many ways, been so perfect on paper. The right background, the right job schedule and career goals, similar tastes in movies and games, friends he got along with . . . But their kinks had never quite matched up. There'd always been tension, that little something off. It had never been effortless, and that was the gold standard, wasn't it? Wanting that—the possibility of that—drew his mind back again and again to the feel of Mindy's body against his, the way she'd offered herself, the sounds she'd made that seemed perfectly attuned to his libido.

Because he had willpower, he kept walking. But by the time he reached the front porch, he'd given up on giving it up. He grudgingly took a seat on the creaking swing to the left of the door, making the most of the cooling breeze as he let his mind pick things over. Mindy might stay the week, might not. If she *did*, he needed to have a plan for dealing with her, some kind of attitude he could adopt that would make the whole situation more manageable.

Show her who's boss.

No, no, no . . . Okay, well, *yes.*

Logan was no pickup artist. But he'd had enough management training in his old job to know something about dealing with people, and he knew that you often had to start with whatever dynamic was already there. Mindy might not be a sub, but she reacted like one. And he was a Dom. So what did that natural dynamic tell him to do?

He clamped down on the first several lurid images that came to mind, and cranked his mind back to possibilities that wouldn't shock the other guests. What *flavor* of not-a-sub was Mindy? In the barn she'd been anxious, penitent, and—annoyed as he'd been with her, suspicious though he still was, he had to give credit where it was due—not actually a brat. She never had been one of those. Thinking back, he recalled her in high school. Cheerleading, but also driving over to Kerrville to volunteer at the hospital. And part of the group that went to the elementary schools to read to the little kids. Even now, the thing with her stepfather—she was spirited, enthusiastic, but almost ridiculously eager to please.

Service sub. Or rather . . . a *person* who liked service. Liked to have a job to do, to feel she was helping somebody. Maybe even liked to lose herself in that a little. He could use that. Put her to work—using the fact that she was an old high school friend to excuse his presumption to the other guests, if necessary. She would feel useful, he would get some free work out of it, and if it wasn't entirely ethical on his part . . . well, she would never know he was kind of getting off on it, would she? And if she didn't like it, she could always leave. Nothing skeezy about that. As a bonus, sending her on little errands around the place would also get her out of his sight for chunks of time. Depending, of course, on the errands.

If circumstances were different, he would send her out to cut her own switch. Then have her bring it to him, present it, present herself. He could almost see the brilliant ladder of marks he would leave with a slender wand of oak, almost feel the resistance of her creamy skin as he slapped the wood in a careful, symmetrical pattern. It was tricky not to break the skin with a switch, and splinters were a concern, so he'd have to resist the follow-through. Although maybe, just at the end, right across the sweetest curve of her beautiful ass, he'd let it fly. Make *her* fly. Cut through the surface and let her know she'd paid in full for whatever she'd done. And then he'd fuck her until he couldn't see straight.

The disgruntled ache in his groin reminded him this train of thought was going nowhere helpful. Well, maybe he wasn't ten kinds of fool after all. He was mostly only one: the kind who thought with his dick.

Sighing, he pushed off with his feet, setting the swing in motion again, and tried to think about the ranch's profit-and-loss statements instead of Mindy Valek's ass.

"You and me, Moose. You and me."

The spider didn't answer. He seemed content to hang in his web, scarcely moving. There were already some rips and suspiciously lumpy spots in the gossamer, so she assumed Moose had fed for the evening.

She really didn't want to sleep with him in the cabin, but since the alternative seemed to be heading to the main house for assistance . . .

"You just stay on your side, dude. Invisible wall, right here." She gestured, knowing it was pointless, but still too much a child of the media to completely rule out that the spider might somehow understand. Moose might come to cartoon life in the night, to croon supportive lullabies. Or weave her a magical garment. Who was she, in her heart of hearts, to deny the power of these fantasies?

On the other hand, it was a Texas spider—a big, fat, small-town good ol' boy—so more likely it would come to life spouting misogyny and burping up a Shiner. She didn't want to be in *that* cartoon. But she'd chance it rather than risk running into Logan again.

Mindy's stomach growled, reminding her of the dinner she'd skipped. *Stupid.* Stubborn, because she did plan to stay the week. But stupid, because she knew all it would lead to was hopeless fantasizing.

Logan. Those stern, steely eyes. The leather around her wrist, his hands strong and irresistible as he secured her to the shelf bracket. Shivering, Mindy raised a hand to her face, touching the stubble burn by her lower lip and sighing—then covering her mouth as though silencing herself could somehow stifle the imagery in her brain. Or the memory of the smells—the leather, the saddle soap, the hay and sweet oats, the *eau de Logan* she could still detect on her own T-shirt.

Possibly that part was in her own head. There was no way his scent could linger longer than horse. But wasn't the mindfuck the most powerful kind?

Her own imagination lent Logan powers she knew he probably didn't have. Even better bondage skills, for instance. She'd already mentally revised the barn scenario, tossing out the mismatched restraints to feature leather ties on both wrists, and halter ropes securing her ankles to . . . something. Didn't matter. It was going in the spank bank, ranking right up there with the impersonal-Dominant-stranger-in-the-motel-room-with-the-businessman-friend fantasy. She wasn't *proud* of that, but she wasn't going to apologize or lie to herself, either. That ten minutes or so in the barn with Logan Hill had been so hot she was still reeling from it.

Or maybe that was the hunger. Her stomach roared audibly, and Mindy growled back at it. There was no way she'd make it through the night. And she didn't have so much as a granola bar in her purse.

"*Shit.*"

In theory, guests were welcome in the main kitchen between meals—it had been part of the grand tour. There were chips and fruit to snack on, and cold cuts for sandwiches. A big cooler of soda and water bottles. All part of the down-home charm. Logan had never stated a closing time. Probably an oversight on his part, but still, it wasn't even ten o'clock yet. Picking up the flashlight, she stepped out the front door and glanced up the trail to the top of the hill. Lights were still on at the big house. They beckoned, whispering to her of warmth and food.

Deciding to chance it, she locked the door behind her and flicked the flashlight on. A few yards away, a startled armadillo scuffled off the path into the scrub. It was unusual to see a live one, and she wondered if it was a good or bad omen.

Bad, she decided retroactively as she hit the trailhead and scanned across the wide yard to the main house's front porch. Even facing mostly away, obscured by the porch pillar and the back of the swing, Logan was clearly recognizable by his blue plaid shirt and his golden-blond hair. Ridiculous how it formed gentle waves wherever it was long enough, but didn't seem to frizz. And his eyelashes, long and dark despite his blond coloring, while her own were so pale they were practically invisible without mascara. Unfair things. But life was full of those.

A ruthless landman would be standing there in the darkness, contemplating how to turn the whole situation into the ideal negotiation. Use the casual setting to disarm the other party. Find common ground. Learn what they needed, what they were lacking. But really, all Mindy could think about was the prospect of a sandwich. Probably the cutthroat businessperson should remember to pack emergency granola bars.

She was halfway across the yard when he spotted her, and a thick blanket of awkwardness fell over the scene as he watched her approach. She expected him to stand—good manners and all that—but apparently he was done with cordiality for the night. At the bottom step she stopped, feeling like she was petitioning for entrance to the inner sanctum. If she'd made it across the side yard unseen she could have detoured toward the side of the house and gone in through the kitchen door with nobody the wiser, but probably this encounter was inevitable. It had that feeling.

"Mindy. What do you need?"

So. Definitely done with cordiality.

"I wanted to know if I could still get a sandwich?" When he just lifted his eyebrows, looking mildly surprised, she reminded him, "I skipped dinner."

"Right." Reluctantly, he stood and opened the door for her, gesturing her through.

She couldn't resist a sniff as she passed him, but only caught the faintest hint of the smell that had lingered so tantalizingly on her shirt earlier. It was all she could do to resist rubbing a hand across his chest, or leaning her forehead there the way she had earlier, when she'd cried like such an idiot.

Logan seemed quieter now, more aloof than angry, and she felt his eyes on her as she led the way down the hall to the back of the house where the kitchen was located. She could hear movement elsewhere in the house, the sound of somebody typing, a television or something with the sound down low. But the kitchen was empty, only one industrial-style fixture over the giant farmhouse sink illuminating the space. The long butcher-block island was spotless, the stainless counters shone dully from the shadows, all the dishes were neatly stowed on shelves.

"If the kitchen's closed, I can—"

"You need to eat." He put a hand on her hip and gently nudged her from the doorway, then reached for the light switch, turning on the under-cabinet lights. "Ham, salami, or turkey?"

He washed his hands before retrieving ingredients from the big commercial fridge, shooting options at her the whole time. Ham on rye, no cheese, no tomato. Mayo, mustard. Lettuce, sure, why not? Yes to onions, because they were kind of a statement that she didn't expect any further kissing to happen.

When all the components were out on the counter, he pulled down two plates and gestured to her, clearly expecting her to take over.

"Oh, you want me to . . . um, sure. Just let me . . ." Late to the party, she washed her hands, then turned to the task of assembling both her own sandwich and a second one for Logan. She was nearly done by the time she realized she was actually *making him a sandwich*, not really what she'd planned for the evening. He'd already eaten dinner, presumably. But then he was a big guy—tall, rangy—

and probably ripped through calories at a furious pace. Dude was probably hungry all the time.

He watched her as she worked, and he *looked* hungry, to the extent she could bring herself to watch him back. Something about his face—the stern expression, probably—made her look down automatically, made her *bow her head*. If he hadn't tied her up earlier, she might never have drawn the connection, but now she was thinking of him like a Dom, *dammit*, and she couldn't get her body to stop responding accordingly.

That didn't mean she was okay with him tricking her into making him a sandwich, though. When she was done, she slid him the plate with a frown. "Mild coercion on rye, side of gender stereotype."

"My favorite." He picked up the sandwich, not bothering to hide his grin. "Right outside that door is a whole world of consent, and nobody is stopping you." He took a huge bite and munched, still smiling.

She wished she could lose her appetite and stalk out, but it was far too late for that. She tucked into her own sandwich and suppressed a moan. It was really good ham, and the onions were the sweet kind. Heaven. As she chewed, she pondered what he'd said, the fact that he'd responded to the coercion charge by countering with consent. *Interesting.*

It wouldn't actually be so hard, would it, to find out whether he was kinky? Just drop a few key words and see if he picked up on it? *If I say "safe," you say . . .*

But did she really want to know? Would that make things better or infinitely worse?

There he stood, leaning on the island, sexy even while taking a far-too-large bite from his rapidly dwindling sandwich. The only safe part about him was her assumption that he was as vanilla as a cream soda. Without that . . .

A gentle throat-clearing broke the silence; Robert was leaning into the kitchen from the hallway, his feet still beyond the door frame.

"May I come in, sir?"

"*Robert.*"

"Boss."

"Yes. Come on in."

Robert floated past, clearing the plate from in front of Logan and then swinging by to pick up hers before carrying both to the sink.

Startled, she realized she'd finished her sandwich. She glanced at Logan, who was biting the side of his cheek and studiously staring up at the central light fixture.

And . . . that was that, then. *Sir*. And permission. And if she hadn't been there, she'd be willing to lay odds Robert would've engaged in a lot more protocol than that. Logan might be a subtle Dom, if he was one, but Robert was far from a subtle bottom. He had a rainbow key fob latched to his right-hand belt loop, and wore a thick metal choker-length necklace she'd assumed from the start was a street collar.

That in itself hadn't meant much, because it wouldn't have flagged him to anyone not already kinky. But the fact that Logan had corrected his "sir," that he had tied her up for what should have been a business conversation, had been so quick with an assurance about consent . . . too much smoke for there not to be a fire.

And Lord, was there ever fire. She would probably regret confirming his status, because she would out herself in the process, and it would give him a certain amount of power over her if he was unscrupulous. On the other hand . . . so far, she'd been the unscrupulous one. So maybe by doing this, she would right the balance. Gripping the edge of the island, she exhaled, centering herself, then spoke softly.

"If I say *'safe,'* you say . . . ?"

At the sink, Robert started whistling. The bridge from a certain Rihanna song. Of course. Had she just been willfully blind this whole time?

Logan sighed, shooting a glare over his shoulder at his employee before leveling his gaze at Mindy. She made herself return it without flinching. She wasn't *his* sub.

Finally, after sighing again in clear exasperation, Logan answered. "I say, 'risk-aware.' And I also say it's time for you to go back to your cabin. You'll want to rest up for tomorrow."

Fair enough. She was trembling so hard she was afraid she'd lose the sandwich if she stayed, anyway. "Can I have a Coke to go?"

Little muscles all over Logan's jawline tightened, and his eyes narrowed. "No. You may have a water bottle to go. The cooler's right behind you."

She'd known that. What she didn't know was why she'd asked permission for a Coke.

Liar, liar, pants on fire.

She pulled up the lid, knowing she could take whatever she wanted out of the cooler. Knowing, too, that she would only take a water bottle.

Retrieving her flashlight from the island, she headed for the back door this time. Logan moved behind her, picking up condiments to return to the fridge. Clearing all evidence of their bizarre, revelatory sandwich feast.

Maybe he'd just wanted to be fueled up for the big day tomorrow, whatever that entailed. Funny, she didn't recall anything particular on the schedule. Why should she need to rest up?

With one hand on the knob, she turned to ask him about it. He was stopped next to the fridge, his eyes trained where her ass had been a moment before. Not just looking at it like he appreciated it— looking at it like he owned it.

It should have been awkward. In any normal social context, it would have been. Except he made eye contact, with that stern look back on his face, and made a little pirouette gesture with his hand. Then dropped his eyes again, clearly waiting for her to turn around for him to ogle some more.

The real decision point hadn't been the Coke after all. It was this. Her blood rang in her ears, and she was barely aware of Robert's whistling as he flipped the damp dish towel over his shoulder and sauntered out of the kitchen.

Should she turn around, yank the door open, stalk off in a huff like she undoubtedly *should*? Or . . .

She pivoted slowly on one foot, placed her free hand on the door-knob . . . and stopped.

Logan took a step closer, and she could almost feel the heat of his body, his gaze. Long seconds ticked by. Sweat from the water bottle dripped down Mindy's wrist, dampening the flashlight, as well, making it hard to keep a grip on both. Would he touch her?

"Back around."

She hadn't ever thought of herself as having an inspection kink. But when she turned around, Logan kept staring, and this time she knew he wasn't waiting to check out her ass. His eyes were trained on her pussy, pulling a flush from her. She wasn't wet enough for it to show through her jeans, but it felt that way, an instant surge of crazy hormonal activity as her body responded to his attention. By the time his eyes lifted up to the level of her chest, her nipples were hard, clearly visible through her bra and T-shirt. Nowhere to hide. She dropped her gaze to the floor at last, unable to resist the internal pressure.

She might as well have been naked, he'd undressed her with his eyes so effectively. Naked would have felt more comfortable, in a way. More anonymous. Naked, in a club, with black-painted walls and a dungeon master standing nearby in an orange safety vest. This interaction in a kitchen, fully clothed, with a guy she'd known since high school, felt . . .

Filthy.

Perfect.

"Did you have something else you wanted to ask me, Mindy?"

Did she? It had been burned from her consciousness, if so. He'd looked at her for a few seconds and turned her into a column of pure, pent-up need. There was nothing else but that. She shook her head. "I . . . no."

"No . . . ?"

She exhaled, not quite a laugh, but the whole thing seemed so surreal she couldn't help herself. Still, there was no way she could *not* say it. She could at least meet his eyes when she did, though. They both knew what her answer meant. She forced her eyes back up. Logan held her gaze and lifted an eyebrow, and Mindy felt a blush spread from her chest to her cheeks. "No, *sir.*"

He nodded, a smile turning his lips up for a second, and with an almost sickening jolt, Mindy recognized a rush of pride, a sense of accomplishment. For having pleased him in some way. *Oh, I am so fucked.*

"Well, I guess that pretty much answers any remaining questions I had, too." Then he turned away, clearly dismissing her even before he spoke again. "Good night, Mindy."

Chapter Six

What the hell have I gotten myself into?

She'd been asking herself that all day, while eating history's most awkward breakfast with the rest of the guests and a host with whom she could not make eye contact. While smiling to cover her moment of *Whaaaaat...* when Logan had cheerfully announced to the group that his "old friend" Mindy would be helping the staff out for the week, so the other guests should feel free to rely on her. While hauling saddle after saddle from the tack room, and doing whatever else Lamar could foist off, including "shadowing" Thelma Gordon on the trail ride just in case she fell off the plodding, amiable gelding Lamar had assigned her.

Not that there was much danger. Logan had led the pack of guests up what the brochure called the "Low Trail," and Logan and his brother, Ethan, called the "Bunny Slope." Wide enough to accommodate a truck, neatly groomed, so even Mindy thought she could have Rollerbladed along it except for the gentle rise.

The greatest hazard was the risk that one of the placid trail horses would decide to stop for a graze, or be startled by a darting rabbit or lizard. That didn't happen. And despite a few close calls, Thelma didn't fall off.

The ride itself wasn't exactly a hardship. The weather was behaving, staying in the sunny low eighties, and the views from up in the hills were spectacular. Lush vistas of wildflowers and granite, the soothing jostle of the horses, the unaccustomed exercise. The outside world slipped away, replaced with beauty and simplicity and the need to be physically present and alert to the now. It was almost better than a night at the club.

Almost.

By the time they made the two-hour-long loop and returned the horses to Lamar at the stable, Mindy realized there was another similarity to a night at the club: Her ass was sore. But her dream of a long soak in her cabin's cute claw-foot tub was thwarted by Thelma Gordon and her husband, Floyd.

"Mindy, Mr. Hill said they have some maps back at the big house, and you'd be the person to ask about where to go shopping in town."

Logan, who was just dismounting behind the charming couple, shot a shit-eating grin her way. "Maps are on the sideboard in the entryway. You remember where, right, Mindy?"

Bastard.

The Gordons were waiting for a response.

"I'd be happy to help. Were you interested in souvenirs, or maybe antiquing, or . . . ?"

"No souvenirs." Floyd tugged his hat further down on his forehead with a look of determination.

Thelma patted his upper arm. "Maybe just something for the grandkids. Let's look at what they have down there."

Half an hour later—armed with more knowledge about the Gordons' grandchildren than she could have ever asked for, and having described the relative merits of just about every business establishment she could remember in town—Mindy escaped the main house and the delightful Gordons, only to run smack into Ethan. Logan's little brother had arrived early that morning with a loaded horse trailer and a lot of enthusiasm. Mindy thought the ranch could use the infusion of knowledge and energy, but she was leery when he turned the slightly manic gleam in his eyes her way.

"Hey, just the person I was looking for!"

Her heart sank. The long soak in the bath was never to be. "Oh?"

"Yeah, Logan said you'd offered to help with the fire pit. The rocks just got delivered. If we get it all set up this afternoon, there should be plenty of time for the cement to cure, and we can have some campfire time before the end of the week."

He grinned, clearly not expecting "no" for an answer. Mindy stifled a groan. "Campfire time? Awesome! Can we toast marshmallows?"

Ethan leaned forward and winked. "And sing songs, Mindy. *Cowboy songs.* Diego plays the git-tar. It's gonna be so great."

She nodded. "Yippee-kai-yay."

He nodded right back. "Motherfucker."

They held it for a second, then lost it, cracking up, holding each other for support until they laughed themselves out. Finally Ethan pushed away and shrugged. "He's roped us both into it, he has his ways. But the only solution is to have some fun with it, am I right? I plan to write all kinds of stuff in the mortar layers and bake my opinion right into the damn thing."

That thought cheered her tremendously. She followed him toward the soon-to-be fire pit area with a lighter heart. "It'll make the marshmallows taste that much sweeter."

So with some borrowed work gloves and a lot of elbow grease, she spent the rest of the afternoon helping to haul fire-safe bricks and rocks from the parking lot to the level spot near the cabin trailhead.

Not the saddle-soreness cure she had desired. But almost certainly better for her character.

Mindy hated things that were good for her character. But she was a sucker for feeling useful. These two traits often collided with exhausting results.

The worst part—sort of—was knowing Logan was watching her. Judging her. She hated him for it, but she hated herself a lot more for the circumstances leading up to it. She wanted to make up for what she'd done. Every rock she carried, staggering, to the rapidly growing circular pit, felt like a weight lifted from her shoulders. As the afternoon progressed, she felt Logan's attention shift from glowering disapproval to grudging admiration, and it restored a piece of her soul. Lamar was slower to come around, but even he was less gruff by late afternoon.

Manual labor and domestic discipline were not kinks of Mindy's, but that day she understood the appeal. Do a bad, make a good. Right the balance.

It was still no fun when she dumped off what she thought was her last paving stone and Logan pointed back to the parking lot with his mortar-slathered trowel. "Two more."

The fire pit area had been leveled and covered in landscape fabric a few weeks earlier, when Lamar and Diego had poured the concrete base for the pit. Wide stone benches surrounded it—pulled, Ethan explained, from the overgrown garden behind the main house. Restoring *that* was a project for another time, apparently.

When Mindy made her *actual* last heavily laden trudge from the parking lot, Lamar and Diego had left the fire pit. Robert had departed long since to start on dinner. The sun was lowering, and Mindy was starving. She collapsed on one of the benches and watched Ethan and Logan mortar the final two capstones into place.

Ethan slapped his trowel down next to the mortar bucket with a weak but triumphant "Yaaaay." Then he slumped dramatically backward, sprawling on the landscape fabric.

"Gotta finish cleaning up." Logan poked his leg with his toe. "C'mon, man."

Ethan lifted his head only enough to shake it. "Fuck that. I'm taking a break. Or joining a stronger union."

"Ugh. Mindy." Logan gestured toward the trowel, then glanced at his brother. He seemed to be taking a moment to evaluate his approach before he looked back at her. "Will you please take that and rinse it off before it's ruined? There's a faucet and hose on the front side of the house to the right of the stairs behind the bushes."

She knew she should just do it. Part of the penance. But he'd asked so politely instead of just telling her, because he hadn't wanted to order her around in front of Ethan. It left her an opening she couldn't resist. "Naaaah. I think I'm about done here, if you don't mind. That last trip from the parking lot wiped me out. Gonna sit for a few minutes and chill until Robert rings the dinner bell."

"Ohhhh," Ethan said from the ground, "there's *subtext*. So much subtext. You two, seriously. Hey, Mindy, I hear you're working as a landman now? How's that going for you?"

Sigh. "Oh, it's awesome. How's that whole vet thing?"

"Stellar. Gets me all the chicks."

As one, Logan and Mindy said, "Gross, dude." They glanced at each other and then away again, quickly.

Ethan lifted his head, stared at them each in turn, then lowered it again, lacing his hands behind his neck. "Speaking of gross, or actually of being officially *not* gross . . . bro, did you finally get that Healthvana problem sorted out?"

Logan coughed. Mindy's ears pricked. She had a current clean bill of health on the app herself. Did Logan have an unpleasant secret?

He blushed—or it might have been the result of too much afternoon sun and labor. "Ethan. Not okay. Boundaries."

"What? Health is important."

"We're with somebody I know in a . . . professional context. That isn't . . . you don't just . . . no. I mean, yes, I got it sorted out. But you don't go implying . . . I mean, now I have to—"

"I don't need to know," Mindy hastened to reassure him. "No big deal."

"It's this app where you can—"

"I know, I know. I have it. Because, you know, a lot of play parti—private clubs, they . . . aw, fuck." Private sex clubs. Really professional topic of conversation. For super-professional grown-ups. She might as well have strolled through the barnyard in nothing but a corset and heels.

Ethan propped himself on his elbows, grinning. "Oh, do go on."

She shot him a look. "You're a terrible human being. You didn't *seem* this terrible growing up. I have negatives all the way down. So there."

"I do, *too*," Logan said. "I had a password issue with my clinic. My results weren't getting updated. My brother"—he gave Ethan more than just a toe-nudge—"is just being a dick. He needs to learn to exercise some damn restraint."

Ethan shrugged, then eased his long, lean body up from the ground with unexpected grace. "I could teach you a thing or two about restraint, as you well know." He didn't seem sorry at all. In fact, he started whistling as he picked up the trowel and sauntered off toward the front of the house.

Mindy was so used to a situation where her face was on fire and others were calm. It was intriguing to see Logan—toppy, confident Logan—navigate that particular set of feelings. On the whole, she didn't like it. It didn't feel like justice at all.

She nodded in Ethan's direction. "Gee, he seems nice."

Logan rolled his eyes and shook his head. "He's fine. He can be a jerk sometimes, but he doesn't mean any harm by it. Mostly he just thinks he knows best about people and feelings and he wants it to all be out in the open. Thinks that's easier."

"He's not necessarily wrong." *But.* "Did he think we have something going on that needs to be out in the open?"

He chuckled sheepishly and took his hat off, rubbing his hand over his hair. "Uh, maybe? I might have . . . expressed some frustration in a way that led him to believe that was a possibility. Not on purpose, he just picks up on stuff. He always has. And once he found out I was kinky, too, it only got worse."

"Too? Oh . . . the restraint thing. I get it." Kinksters everywhere. First Logan and Robert, now Ethan. It was turning out to be quite the kinky dude ranch.

"He's really good with ropes. If you ever know anyone who likes to be tied up, he really seems to know his stuff." He flipped his hat a few times with his fingertips, then popped it back onto his head.

"Okay, he's your brother, though," she pointed out, "so this is kind of a weird area."

"For you and me both. You have no idea. He's really not great at boundaries."

Mindy recalled Ethan as a brilliant student, but one of those kids who always seemed to contain too much energy for the space they occupied. She didn't know if it was hyperactivity or what, but he'd always been either literally bouncing off the walls, or so absorbed in a project that he tuned everything else out. His Future Farmers of America animals always won prizes, though—his name was often on the school marquee for that, or in the local paper—so she wasn't surprised he'd become a vet.

Logan had his phone out, scrolling, frowning at the screen. After a second he realized she was looking at him, and he started to put it away then shrugged and turned the screen toward her. "For what it's worth."

A series of minus signs. He was indeed as disease-free as the app could prove. After a second of consideration she pulled her phone from her pocket, pulled the app up, and let him see her results. Why, she wasn't sure. Because they weren't angling to sleep with each other or anything. That would be wildly inappropriate. But it was good to know they'd both been telling the truth.

"He's not wrong," she repeated as she put her phone away. "It is better to have things out in the open."

Logan seemed to consider it a second, then nodded. "Right now, I think it's time to be open about being hungry as fuck, and head in to dinner."

She smiled. "I'll be open about needing some Tylenol and a hot bath. I'm beyond saddle-sore. It's so tragic."

"Been too long?"

"Waaaayyy too long."

"Now you're just teasing." He chuckled and gestured for her to lead the way up to the main house.

She had been teasing—she didn't seem able to help herself. And she had been open about the saddle-soreness, but she felt like she was being secretive about everything that mattered most.

So much jerking off. Logan was considering writing a little song about it, something he could sing to himself like a mantra to calm the insanity.

Once last night, shortly after the guests were tucked in for the evening. He'd made a beeline for his room and the private sanctity of his bathroom, and it was just lucky for him Robert had turned out the lights and locked up. Then a nearly wet dream around two in the morning. He'd woken before the critical moment, thought, *Fuck it*, and finished things off with his hand and a crystal-clear image of that whole scene in the kitchen—only with Mindy naked, her perky butt crosshatched with red from a switching.

By the time he'd hit the shower at 5 a.m., it had seemed inevitable. The naked Mindy in his mind preceded him, knelt under the spray, waited for him to give it up in her mouth—which he did in an embarrassingly short time. That was just his life now, he guessed, jerking off to thoughts of Mindy the Actual Submissive.

For all that, he really would have been fine—if Mindy hadn't been saddle-sore.

She kept *wincing*, was the thing. And putting a hand to her ass when she thought nobody was looking. And avoiding sitting down. And the whole thing was so exactly like the way a sub would act the day after a heavy scene that Logan wanted to react just as he would in that scenario. Specifically, he wanted to walk up behind her and pinch the hell out of that sore flesh and relish every gasp and whimper she tried to stifle. He wanted to find the exact spot that hurt the most and *press it* when she couldn't get away. Then remind her of all the wicked things he'd done the night before to make her that sore, and how clearly he remembered every single bruise and welt, no matter how modestly she might be dressed at the moment. If, that is, he'd been the one to cause the pain, instead of a horse.

Even worse, the worst of all, was when he realized her surreptitious ass pats weren't an attempt to massage the pain away. She was pushing her fingers into the flesh and leaning into the pressure, and at least once he caught the expression on her face when she did it. Rapt, blushing, all but biting her lip. Then looking around, making sure nobody had noticed what she was doing. She liked the pain itself. Seemed—unless Logan's radar was completely broken—to be getting off on it.

Nobody noticed. The whole crowd—five guests, with Ethan breaking trail ahead of them—were focused entirely on the wildlife. It was a birding-and-wildflower-spotting hike, and everybody else was actually watching the birds and looking at the foliage. Mindy was lost in her own world of furtive pain-slut gratification, and Logan was having trouble paying attention to *anything* other than Mindy's butt as she struggled up the rough trail. He was bringing up the rear, but his focus was definitely on only one rear in particular.

Robert and Diego, manning the coolers and grill at the "campfire" destination the guests had been hiking toward, might have had a clue. But they appeared too busy to care that the newest unofficial staff member only stayed at the picnic table long enough to devour a burger, then jumped right back up.

Soothing ointment. That was probably what Logan ought to be offering her. Some Epsom salts for her bath. Some more Tylenol, maybe. Normal things.

Nope, no use. He wanted to apply the soothing ointment *himself,* with Mindy naked, facedown, over his lap. After some additional beating. And probably with no soothing ointment, because really, that would be defeating the purpose. She clearly wanted the pain. He wanted to give her more of it. As much as she could take.

A service-oriented submissive who was a pain slut? With an ass straight out of his dreams and a smile he couldn't help but find adorable, no matter how hard he tried? At least as far as the kinky side of things was concerned—and he couldn't think past that side right now—she was everything he'd longed for and more. All the things he'd been missing.

He lasted all the way through finishing his burger and throwing his paper plate in the garbage bag hanging from a tree near the grill. On the other side of that tree, pretending to consult her laminated quick-reference guide to Central Texas wildflowers, was Mindy. With one hand in her back pocket.

Gripping.

Too much. It was too damn much.

From where Logan stood, a few feet away from Mindy, he could see that the tree trunk and his own body would provide all the shielding he needed. He scanned the handful of guests. Ethan was entertaining them with a story, and they all seemed enthralled. Sufficient distraction to buy him a few seconds.

It would be a gamble, though. And he ought to strike while the iron was hot. Mentally crossing his fingers, he murmured just loud enough for Mindy to hear him, but not Robert or Diego.

"Don't turn around. And don't make a sound unless you want me to stop."

She froze—except for the slight trembling of the hand that held the field guide. "I . . ."

He gave it a second, to make sure she wasn't going to follow up. When she exhaled without saying anything further, he took the final step, closing the distance between them and pulling her hand from her pocket, letting it fall to her side. He smoothed his hand down the curve of her ass until he could grasp the fleshiest part of it between his forefinger and thumb—right where the denim was softest and most faded, at the spot where buttock and thigh met. He pressed, not enough to hurt, and paused.

"Nod if you want me to do it."

She bobbed her head twice, almost before he'd finished his sentence. When he squeezed his fingers together, he heard the air hiss between her teeth as she processed the pain. Heard the tiniest beginning of a moan, so quickly swallowed he could have almost thought he'd only imagined it—if he hadn't know what it was. If he hadn't felt it himself in his lower belly and groin. Mindy started to rise to her toes, bowing her head in counterpoint, and he released her so suddenly she almost fell over.

"You about ready to head back?" he asked more conversationally, crossing his arms to resist further temptation and stepping past her toward the mesquite scrub she'd been pretending to examine a few moments earlier.

"Yeah." High-pitched, breathy squeak of a voice.

Logan chanced a look back at her face. *Big mistake.* Her eyes were closed, her soft, light lashes fanned down and pointing toward the delicate blush illuminating her cheekbones. She looked like a sunset. And he was *desperate* to fuck her.

Over her still-trembling shoulder, Logan could see the two couples and one extra woman—he needed to figure out how to remember all their names—standing, stretching. The pair who had also gone on the trail ride the day before were seasoned riders who hadn't felt a twinge this morning. The Gordons, saddle-sore like Mindy, had opted out of the hike.

Logan had insisted Mindy come along. She hadn't argued very hard against it, and now he could guess why.

"Masochist," he whispered at her as he strode back toward the tables.

She laughed as if she'd been caught off guard, and called her response to him aloud. "Duh."

He turned around, raising his eyebrows, noting then studiously ignoring Robert's snort in his direction. Yeah, that particular ship of gossip had clearly already sailed. Logan tried to stare Mindy down with a cold Dom face but could feel himself failing miserably. She was just too *cute* to glare at.

But he could still call her out. "Brat."

The budding smile melted from her lips, and her eyebrows flew up in the middle like a cartoon face illustrating worry. She shook her head, then lowered her gaze to his boots. "*No. I'm really not.*" She added, "sir," in a whisper he would never have caught if he hadn't been expecting it.

Well, that wouldn't do. "Hey, look up."

She looked up, her eyes scanning past him as if she was recalling their potential audience. Her sheepish grin was too wooden to pass as natural.

He gave her what he sincerely hoped was a reassuring smile. But his heart was in his throat. If he offered, and she said no, he really didn't know how he'd walk away after misreading her so badly. "Nod if you're gonna prove it to me later."

She licked her lips, blinked a few times . . . and nodded.

Oh, her ass was *so* his.

Chapter Seven

Later, he'd said. Prove she wasn't a brat, *later*.

Mindy had assumed he meant later that day, probably after dinner. *Later*, later. The anticipation would have practically been as good as foreplay. But Logan apparently wasn't content to allow anticipation.

He'd started on the walk back down the hill.

The lineup was the same going down as it had been coming up—Ethan leading the way, with Mary more or less by his side asking about the flora and fauna. The Jacksons following, and after them the couple whose names Mindy couldn't recall but felt too embarrassed to ask for again. Then Mindy. Then Logan.

Right behind her. Plotting.

She assumed he was scoping her ass, and she was cool with that. She wondered whether his pinch—*Lordy*, the man had some long, strong fingers—had left a bruise. Some kind of lingering mark. If it hadn't, maybe he would do something else to leave marks. *Later*.

But later came sooner than expected, in the form of a tap on her hip. She looked down, startled, reaching to brush away whatever had landed there, only to find it was the tip of a stick. Or really, more like a switch. She glanced over her shoulder. Logan held the switch at arm's length, keeping a distance between them. He must have grabbed the slender branch and stripped the leaves off it as they walked.

"Eyes front," he told her. "You wouldn't want to trip."

Reluctantly, she turned her head and tried to focus on the trail. On a nearby rock formation. On the plaid shirt and white straw cowboy hat of the guest she was walking behind. On a grackle in the nearest tree, hopping up a few branches as the group passed by. On anything other than the looming possibility of whatever Logan might decide to do to her already aching haunches with the switch.

Gentle taps, at first. A touch here, a slap there, at irregular intervals. He was gauging the distance, it seemed like. And probably the potential for noise. They couldn't do anything to draw attention to themselves, to alert the other guests that anything was happening. Mindy couldn't make a sound no matter what Logan did, she knew that much. She didn't have to be told that even a squeak would end the game.

It was a recklessly stupid game, but she didn't want it to end.

The first harder tap came lower than she expected, right across the back of her left thigh. The denim of her jeans blocked some of the sting, but not all, and tears sprang up as quickly as the heat between her legs. A faint whipping sound announced the next one, over the seat of her pants. She clenched her teeth and kept walking, praying the others hadn't heard the *swish*. Nobody turned around. Ethan had started talking again, about the likelihood of spotting various owls if anyone was interested in a short post-dinner nature stroll.

A truck engine rumbled in the distance—possibly Robert and Diego taking supplies from the picnic ground back to the main compound. The noise masked any warning sound for the next blow, a stripe of fire over her right hip. She exhaled sharply, biting her lips to keep silent.

Gravel crunched louder behind her as Logan approached. Wary eyes on the backs of the others, he muttered at her quickly, "Hook your thumbs in your front belt loops, I don't want to hit your hands."

He was even sexier when he was being practical. *Unfair.* He dropped back and she slid her thumbs into her belt loops and waited. But not for long.

A burning stroke on her hamstring. Another on her butt. Then a pair of searing swishes, back and forth across her waistline, inches above the protection offered by the denim. She stumbled, catching herself before she fell, and Logan was by her side again in an instant, a hand on her shoulder.

The guy in the hat—Gene? Jeff? Jerry?—turned and gave her an encouraging nod. "You doin' okay back there?"

She gave him a thumbs-up. "Fine, fine. All good. Tripped over my own foot. Too busy looking for birds to watch where I'm going, I guess."

Logan patted her shoulder then his hand fell away. She resisted the urge to grab it and put it back. Hat Man was already staring into the trees again, oblivious to the kinky scene he'd nearly witnessed playing out a few yards behind his back.

Not a scene, she corrected herself. This was nothing so involved. They were just screwing around. Playing, not *playing*. Specifically, Logan was fucking with her head because he knew he could, and she was letting him because . . . because she liked it, but in the circumstances she could lie to herself a little bit and pretend it was because she felt guilty about the whole trying-to-seduce-his-ranch-out-from-under-him deal.

It wasn't *entirely* a lie. She did want to atone. But the pain was melting into warmth, into pleasure, the new sharper spots pulling focus from the all-over achy tension of the saddle-soreness. Mindy could *feel* everything, feel every inch of her damaged skin as if it were being stroked. The friction of her snug jeans over her crotch was nearly too much; her pussy and clit were so sensitive and ready that even the act of walking seemed like enough stimulation to make her come.

Or maybe that was the weight of Logan's assessment. She could feel him, too, sizing her up. She wished they were alone on this trail, that she was naked, that he was switching her back to the barn to tie her up in the tack room again. Or cross-tie her in the open corridor between the stalls, maybe. Where he would fuck her roughly. Then he would wash her off as gently as he would any of the other livestock, before bedding her down for the night in a stall.

She was so caught up in the unexpectedly hot sex-pony fantasy she forgot to anticipate the next swat. Straight up between her legs, fast as a rattlesnake strike, not so much hard as purely startling.

"*Oh.*"

Logan cleared his throat, and she bit her lip again. *Shit.*

Her legs were trembling. At this rate, she was never going to survive the last fifteen minutes of the hike without falling flat on her face. She turned quickly and made a slashing motion across her throat, then shrugged an apology.

Logan didn't play fair. Not one little bit. He pushed his bottom lip out into a pout. And then, *and then*, the absolute rat bastard made puppy-dog eyes at her. *On purpose.*

It was horrifyingly effective. It took every bit of steel in her not to turn back around and let him do whatever he wanted. Although the fact she was still horny enough to hump his leg might have played a part. She mouthed a clear *"no"* instead, flicking her gaze forward only long enough to make sure she wasn't about to walk into a tree or granite boulder or coral snake or something. The trail held only oblivious guests and snake-free dust.

When she looked back to Logan he sighed, exaggerating that every bit as much as he had the pout, and held up the switch in both hands, clearly about to break it in half. That would never do.

She echoed his pout and soulful eyes, masterfully suppressing a giggle-snort as she did so.

He grinned and broke the switch anyway, tossing it into the brush. Then he raised his eyebrows at her and if she hadn't already been wet, that would've done it.

Ethan said something enthusiastic about rose poppies, and Mindy dutifully trained her eyes on the swatch of land to the right of the trail, where a scattering of vivid cerise blooms completely stole the show from the few early bluebonnets. Within a few more weeks, the whole thing would probably be bright cobalt and white. Then yellow and red as the season progressed and other flowers had their moments. It was magical, a fairy-tale landscape, lacking only a mythical jackalope to complete the picture.

Maybe the jackalope was hiding right behind that stand of oak trees. Or there could be Hill Country rock fairies crouched atop that limestone ridge. These were smarter, safer fantasies to focus on than the barn sex thing. By the time the group reached the first of the old stone outbuildings near the main house, Mindy had populated the entire place with imaginary playmates.

Logan's voice startled her from her reverie. "Hey, Ethan, I'm gonna stop here. Diego said something about the wall behind the old shelves needing repointing. Mindy, can you help me out for a minute?"

Smooth. The rest of the group didn't bat a collective eye, they were all so eager to get back to their cabins or whatever else now that the hike was at an end.

Logan worked the heavy iron latch on the oak door, held it open for Mindy to enter the dim, single-roomed stone building, then closed the latch, securing them inside. A second later he had her back to the wall, his knee between her thighs, his hands gripping her hips like vises.

She expected a kiss, but she didn't get one. Logan studied her face instead, through the gloom, then moved his hands. Pulling her closer, nudging her up his thigh until she was straddling it, almost on her toes. Then rocking her against it, hard. His fingers curved around her ass, pushing her into a rhythm.

"Keep going. Ride me just like that. Don't stop."

"I . . . God. Okay."

He slapped her thigh, hard. "Yes, sir."

"Yes, sir." And *oh*, it felt good to say it.

"Don't come."

His telling her not to made it approximately a thousand times more likely to happen. She ground against his leg, finally letting out the groan she'd been holding back most of the way down the trail. When she squeezed herself around him, her legs sang with pain and her entire body responded.

"I've been rethinking some things," Logan said, raising one hand to lift her shirt in front and yank down the cups of her bra. "Since you're here for a few more days, and it's pretty fucking obvious we're both into it, I think we should throw this professionalism and restraint thing out the window and do all the things we'd like to do instead. What do you think?"

Think? That was the last thing she wanted to do. Thinking might result in making a smart decision, and at the moment Mindy only wanted to make the dumbest possible decision when it came to Logan. She humped his leg harder. "If you throw restraint out the window, we can't do *all* the things I'd like to do. Sir."

He pinched her nipple, hard. "You're not exactly showing me what a brat you're not."

It was almost too much stimulation, nearly enough to put her over the sharp edge she was currently walking. Her orgasm swirled into range, hers for the taking. She wanted it. She wanted his permission more. "I'm sorry, sir." *I'm really not a brat, I'm just at the end of my rope here.*

"You're close, aren't you?" He pinched harder. Mindy nodded, unable to get the words out. Logan made a speculative noise, deep in his throat. "Don't come."

She whimpered, but he just laughed shakily and pulled his leg away. He pointed to the floor.

"Do we need barriers for oral?"

The conversation yesterday suggested strongly there was no need. They were both disease-free, right? She shook her head.

"Good. Knees. Now."

Didn't need to tell her twice. Wincing at the way it abused her already-tortured muscles, she dropped to her knees, breath still coming too fast. *So close.*

"Hands behind your back. Keep 'em there." He ran his thumb over her lips, then pressed the lower one until she opened up. "Good. Stay there. Don't move."

He stepped to the door and double-checked the latch, then walked over to the back wall, where light filtered through an aged four-paned window covered with shutters that more or less matched the door in rough-hewn construction. Each of the shutters had a heart-shaped cutout in the middle, and apparently the view from there revealed the coast was still clear. Logan returned to stand in front of her, sliding two fingers into her mouth, playing with her hair as she suckled.

Mindy's eyes drifted shut. She licked around Logan's fingers, scraping as gently as possible with her teeth. Wanting it to be his cock. This was a place she knew, a role she knew. Why couldn't everything in life be as simple and direct as this?

She wanted him to keep petting her forever, and was sad when his hand left her hair. But the next thing she heard was a belt being unbuckled, and she sighed as a fresh surge of dizzying want swept through her. When he took his fingers out of her mouth, she opened her eyes just enough to watch him unzip his jeans and pull out his cock.

One part of her mind couldn't help but assess it clinically. Cut, average length, nice girth. The other part of her brain had gone primal, overridden by want. Taste, fuck, serve, do whatever he wanted. When he took himself in a firm grip and stroked up and down his length, she licked her lips then opened her mouth a bit wider than before.

Somewhere outside the building, a bird trilled. Inside, the only sound was breathing and the soft *creak* of denim being pushed aside, the scuff of Logan's boot on the dusty stone floor as he stepped in and brought his cock to her lips. She breathed him in, the afternoon smell of him, knowing that musk would linger on her face, marking her as surely as the stripes he'd probably left on her legs and ass.

He didn't need to say it, but he did, as he flexed his hips forward and pushed his tip onto her tongue. "Suck me. Yeah, take my cock."

She hummed around him, swirling her tongue to get him wetter. He didn't give her much time, he put his hands on her head and held her in place and worked his way into her mouth whether she was ready or not. She caught up when he pulled halfway out, licking frantically to get him wetter before he slid back in again, deeper than before. She tasted a hint of pre-come, welcoming the extra lubrication. Her distressed whimpers as she struggled to accommodate him only seemed to excite Logan more; heaven knew the whole situation was exciting Mindy right out of her mind, so that seemed only fair.

"Oh, that's it. You're gonna take all of it." His voice was roughening as he started to pump faster. "Take all of my cock, and then take all my come, like a good little—hmm."

She probably wouldn't have minded whatever he was about to call her, but since they hadn't talked about it beforehand, it was probably just as well. Mindy's knees ached, her lips felt bruised from the rough treatment, and her throat felt tight and scratchy every time Logan thrust deep. Hot need bloomed between her thighs, an ache so keen she didn't know how long she could stand it. But within a few more seconds, Logan's grip tightened in her hair; he forced his cock deeper than ever, and came with a gasp. Spurts of heat bathed the back of Mindy's tongue, and she swallowed desperately, not wanting to miss a single drop.

When he finally slid his cock free, she ducked her head to follow it, but he thwarted her with the fist still in her hair. "No."

Rats.

He tucked himself back in, shaking his leg and grimacing. His damp cock seemed reluctant to settle into place behind clothes. Mindy had little sympathy.

"Okay, up."

She grumbled as she stood, unable to stop herself. Already sore, stiffening, and then made to kneel on stone. It would have been a buzzkill if she hadn't been so primed to begin with.

Oh, who am I kidding? The whole thing is unspeakably hot.

It was. And it got unbelievably hotter when Logan chose that moment to re-roll one of his shirtsleeves that had come loose during their exertions. She stared at his hands and forearms, the cords of muscle running up from his wrists, the blunt tips of his fingers. She remembered what his hands had looked like when he wrapped the leather rein around her wrist to bind it. She wanted to take off all her clothes and fling herself at him, but he didn't give her the chance.

Stepping back in, he shoved his knee between her thighs again, and gave her ass a slap. "Do it. Rub off on me. If you want it, you have to do the work this time."

This time. Oh, she wanted the next time already. She wanted all the times, she wanted to come with his cock inside her, she wanted him to force her to orgasm, she wanted to ride him into oblivion like a wild, wild mustang. But this time would do. She shifted her hips, pressing her clit against him, rocking at a tempo she knew would get her there fast.

Logan apparently thought she needed to get there faster. He tucked her shirt up more firmly, tugging the hem up through her collar then running his fingers along the strained edges of her bra cups. He brushed one nipple, softly at first then harder, tucking his forefinger into his thumb then flicking until Mindy cried out.

"More?"

She nodded, nearly frantic. She was close, so close. "Yes, please. Sir. Please . . . *ohhh.*"

He'd lowered his head and taken the already taut, stinging nipple between his teeth. Just a nip, but enough to make that half of her body vibrate with a sudden, jangling awareness. *More* was good. What he did next was better. Not content with a nibble, he grazed his lips lower to a spot an inch or so below her nipple, winding his arms around her waist and hitching her closer. And then he bit down. Gently at first. Then harder. Then *hard*, so hard she moaned as she tried to breathe through the pain.

It threw her off for a second, as she processed it. Her hips hitched in their pace. Then Logan released her skin, and pressed the tenderest kiss to her nipple again, and she came all at once, pushing against him violently, following each nerve impulse until she had run down every last ounce of pleasure.

Exhausted, spent, she let herself slump against Logan. Soaked in the heat from his body, reveled in the closeness while the endorphins still ruled her. But as her head cleared, the truth sank in. This was basically no better than a one-off scene.

Sure, it was likely to be a few nights . . . and days, apparently. And she already knew Logan. But it was still just like the club, just like scening with any new Dom. Her usual rules needed to apply. Don't assume a great scene means there's a relationship beyond kink. Don't confuse aftercare with love. And the easiest way to avoid that confusion was to avoid a lot of affectionate aftercare.

Logan could glare at her, whip her with a switch, make her carry rocks, make her kneel on the hard stone of this serial killer's playground of a shed while she sucked him off. Those things were fairly straightforward. If she needed it, she might accept water, a warm blanket, even a cup of tea or a snack. But it just wasn't smart to be letting him *cuddle* her.

Chapter Eight

Mindy shivered against him, her body relaxing slowly until she was nestled against his chest. Logan wasn't sure how that had happened, when exactly he'd taken his mouth off her breast and started . . . *snuggling*.

It felt great, though. He was in no hurry for that to be over. Even though he had about a million things to do, details to check on, guests to take care of. Numbers to run. He also did really need to look at the stone wall behind the old shelves. Not that he hadn't fully planned to take advantage of the current situation first. It was madness, really. *Not* the smart way to spend the inaugural weekend of his fledgling business venture. But he just couldn't bring himself to stop. She felt too good, fit too perfectly against him. The whole crazy scene had been that way. Effortless. So damn effortless, like they'd been reading each other's minds.

Mindy pushed away, lifting her head and shaking her hair from her face. "Um."

"Yeah."

She stepped back a pace, her hands the last thing to leave him. One moment pressed flat against his chest, the next dropping to her sides, then crossing awkwardly in front of her. She plucked at her clothes, finally seemed to recall they were askew, and fumbled to pull them back into place.

He called it like he saw it. "You look like you could use a little more snuggling." Yes, good. His body was all in on that plan. Letting her go had been an unexpected loss.

"I'm good. That was awesome. Thank you."

Her tone was polite, but that was all, and Logan had no idea what to do with that. He'd been startled by how good the mini-scene was, and wanted to pursue that further. She'd been so into it when they started. What the hell had happened?

Mindy seemed to recognize that more explanation was needed. She forced her arms down, propping her hands on her hips and rocking up onto her toes a few times. "I mean, it was a good scene, that's all. It was unexpected but fun."

"Okay." It really wasn't okay, but she wasn't wrong, either. It had been a good scene. "Right."

"It wasn't that heavy, so . . . I'm good. And I like to maintain some boundaries."

"Sure. As long as you don't need anything more, after a scene—"

"Well, not after that. That was like thirty percent scene, seventy percent ill-advised beej and dry humping."

Ouch. Still probably not wrong, but she didn't sound like she believed herself. She sounded more like she was afraid he was going to be a dick about things. Like she was protecting herself. He couldn't say that wasn't smart, given the circumstances. There had also been kind of a hate-fucking undertone happening, if he was being honest with himself, so the distance afterward probably made sense objectively. He didn't love that, he'd preferred the snuggling, but it might be all Mindy wanted.

What was he supposed to do? Urge her to accept a hug when she said she didn't want one? She'd already let him switch her until they were both literally panting with need, then sucked him off, then put on an incredible show and gotten him half-hard again. Asking for more right now seemed like it would be more needy than commanding.

And he really *did* have a lot of shit to do.

He clapped his hands, ready for a subject change. "Okay then. So, uh . . . I need to move this shelf and look at the stones. If you want to help, that would be great."

Her confused look was pretty adorable. But Logan was clearly at the stage where he'd find *anything* Mindy did adorable. And not just because of the great blow job. It had started before that. The smiles. The way her hair smelled. The way she hooked her thumbs through her belt loops. The way she sometimes nodded like she was doing the cheerleader head-bob. *Ready? Okay!*

They only had a week. Less than that, because it was already Sunday and she'd be gone on Thursday. It didn't seem like long enough. Not nearly.

"I thought that was just an excuse to get me in here. And possibly add me to your murder list." She grabbed the other side of the rickety shelf and helped him lift it away from the wall.

"Murder list? No, Diego really did want me to check out the mortar." Which, he could clearly see, was flaking away so badly in this spot he was surprised daylight wasn't gleaming through. *Shit.* One more expense.

"Yeah, this shack or whatever looks like, you know . . . the murder hut. The big house looks so normal, and nobody suspects, but then the cops stumble across this and realize you've been wallpapering it all along with cutout pictures of your victims and maybe some— ooh, that's a big spider—maybe some beautiful mind equations or something. Don't kill it!"

"*Don't* kill it?"

"It's probably just an orb weaver. Like Moose!"

"Moose . . . ?"

Mindy looked abashed. "He's my cabinmate. But it's okay. He isn't hurting anything."

The spider scuttled between two stones, and Logan crouched down to scope its escape route. "Daylight. Dammit."

"Do you have to get a stone mason? Are there still stone masons?"

"Here, let's put this shelf back in case Diego decides to use this. Then head back to the house. Yeah, there are still stone masons. Not right in town, but there are a few folks pretty close by. Might have to get somebody from Fredericksburg or somewhere."

"Is it expensive?"

And he remembered why that mattered to her, and he glanced across the shelf at her as they fitted it back against the wall. He had been stupid to let his guard down even for a second. "Do I need to cut another switch?"

She had the grace to look sheepish. "Can't blame a girl for trying. Seriously, though, how are you affording the renovations? I know how much I paid for this trip, I can count the guests and the employees and do the math. My job aside, I do have to wonder."

Logan dusted his hands off on his thighs and crossed to the door, opening it to a flood of unexpectedly bright sunshine. They must have been in the toolshed longer than he'd realized. "After you."

"Oh." She brushed her hands off, echoing his action, then raised them to her face, her hair, as she stepped past him. "Do I look like . . .'

Her lips were rosy and her cheeks flushed. Her hair looked less artfully tousled than it had at the beginning of the day. Nothing she couldn't blame on the sun and wind from the hike. "You look great. How about me?"

"Totes freshly fucked."

He snorted, his moment of irritation vanishing. "That's my aesthetic. And to answer your question, it's part 'using up all my savings and getting help from Ethan and our cousin Chet,' and part 'I have no clue where the rest will come from.' But this week was only ever meant to be a test run. Once the rest of the cabins are fixed up again, and the guest rooms in the main house, we'll be able to take bigger crowds." If they still had any capital left by then, after sinking so much into the money pit the ranch was turning out to be. "The idea is to offer some weekend packages, have different deals for on- and off-season. Start partnering with some local restaurants, maybe try to work with the biker conventions twice a year. And there's also a camping ground, vehicle-accessible. It's on the other side of the hill from where we ate lunch today. Chet thinks we should do RV hookups out there, maybe do some cabin tents, something like that. Also have primitive camping, because he's insane."

"Primitive camping close to a hunting lease seems like an accident waiting to happen."

"*Exactly* what Ethan and I keep telling him. But he says if people can't obey clearly posted warning signs, they have no business stepping outside their homes."

She chuckled. "Sounds like an interesting guy."

"Yeah. He's . . . well. He's one of us."

She gave him that puzzled look, then she got it and nodded. "Must be tough, in Bolero."

Logan shrugged. "It's tough everywhere."

Which was why they were doing this, wasn't it? Sneaking in a beating when nobody was looking. Ducking into hiding spots for some furtive domination and orgasms. Because it was tough to find somebody into kink at all, tougher still to find somebody who seemed to match up perfectly.

And nearly impossible to find the gold standard, the trifecta: somebody who lived close enough for regular scenes, whose kinks aligned with yours, *and* with whom you wanted to spend time outside the kink world.

As they ambled down the trail toward the main house, Logan stole a glance at Mindy. At her messy mop of hair, at her possibly stubble-burned face. He wanted to hold her hand. Instead, he reminded himself that even if they were kink soul mates, she was kind of the devil in disguise.

Clouds were building in the sky as Mindy wound down the road into Bolero Monday morning. In theory, there was a 50 percent chance of thunderstorms. In Central Texas, that could mean anything. The actual weather didn't care about statistics. It might rain none of the time; the clouds would threaten and possibly throw some lightning. It might rain 50 percent of the time, off and on. Or 50 percent of the places, in stripes, one yard left dry while the neighbor's was inundated.

Or it could be an out-and-out deluge. When she'd headed for her car, Lamar had warned of that. Dire and grim, based on his aching knees and overall experience. Mindy figured she'd take her chances. After yesterday's bizarre impromptu toolshed make-out, she needed at least a few hours away from Hilltop Ranch, from Logan, from thinking about her job and how badly she was doing it. The incident had taken the edge off for both of them. Logan had been handling issues with guests the rest of the day yesterday, and had left early that morning with a hunting group, allowing for a cooldown period. Just enough time for doubt to put down some new roots. Mindy needed a distraction, so after lunch she'd set out to see if Bolero could offer her any.

The town looked about like it ever had. Nothing on the outskirts but scattered houses on overgrown acreage. Then a few streets of quarter-acre lots—some with houses, some with trailers, some with businesses. And finally, town proper, a grid of a dozen streets in either direction with a semi-major highway running up the middle. Three traffic-light intersections, up from two back in Mindy's day. The new one was because somebody had died, which was usually what it took to shake the town council on that kind of expenditure. The history was clear from the bright white cross in the grass on the corner. Unnaturally vivid plastic flowers were wired around the horizontal piece and draped around the base. Cheerful colors to mark an awful event.

She stopped into her favorite diner near one end of Main Street. At four in the afternoon it was almost empty, just one old man with a newspaper sitting at the counter and two teenaged boys in the booth farthest from the door. A George Strait song from the eighties was playing, adding to the throwback sensation. The redheaded waitress looked familiar, and turned out to be the younger sister of a girl Mindy had graduated with. The menu looked familiar, too, the same laminated card stock over fading photos of burgers and chicken-fried steak. Mindy ordered a slice of pecan pie and some coffee, and watched the gathering storm through the slightly grubby window as she ate.

She couldn't have counted the number of times she'd sat at this booth at Minnie's Diner, eaten this same pecan pie or a burger, sipped on coffee or a shake, and stared out the window at the clouds. She'd done homework at this table. She'd been on dates here. Broken up with a boyfriend here. Laughed with her friends. Pretended not to cry when she found out about her parents' divorce.

Moving to Dallas had let her reinvent herself. A whole new Mindy, with a new life, a new purpose. She was so much bigger than Bolero; she'd spent years telling herself that, like an affirmation. *If you're nothing else, you're bigger than the Podunk town you came from. You've come so far.* But five minutes sitting on the crackling old red vinyl of a dingy diner booth was all it took to remind her that she hadn't actually *changed*. She hadn't really gone anywhere at all, because the minute she'd sat down she'd felt like she'd come home. That old girl was still here in spirit, which meant a part of her had never left Bolero at all. She could add all the fancy trappings she liked, but she would still be this person. If she didn't know who *this* was, she would never know who she was at all.

Dallas was the dream. Dallas was the fantasy she'd had as a teenager, and she'd made it come to life. But this—this slice of pie at Minnie's Diner, the window overlooking the street and the empty lot between the feed store and the gas station, this gentle, honky-tonk soundtrack—was reality.

Mindy had rejected this reality a long time ago. She might feel authentic sitting in Minnie's and washing her pie down with oversweetened coffee, watching the storm build over the gas station roof, but she had invested a lot of time and effort into the fantasy. An old, broken-in pair of cowboy boots might feel like heaven after a long day, but everybody knew the real value was in the Louboutins you put on so you'd look expensive and people would take you seriously. Even if you'd gotten them on eBay for a hundred fifty dollars, and had to get a cobbler to fix a broken heel before you could wear them.

She should never have come back here. Never put her old boots back on, literally or figuratively. And overlapping kink with what should have been purely about work was the worst decision of all. Risk-seeking behavior, a psychologist might call it. Mindy remembered the term from college psych classes but had never been that type herself. She liked her life in tidy boxes, her danger in easily manageable doses. *Authentic* felt a lot like *everything mashed together*, the good with the bad, the safe with the risky. She didn't want that.

It was time to leave. Not just Minnie's, but Bolero. Hilltop. Logan. The week was a bust, and everything else was a waste of her time— an emotional regression. A set of complications her new, shiny life had no room for.

The clouds tumbled higher and darker, finally losing definition as they compressed into a denser mass. Even in the air-conditioned restaurant, the humidity was palpable. If Mindy had been in shorts, her thighs would have stuck to the vinyl of the booth seat when she tried to stand up after leaving a ten on the table and waving a good-bye to the waitress. When she opened the door, the air hit her like a wall of pea soup, thick and warm. Still, too still—the calm before the storm.

Driving straight back to the ranch to get packed would be the sensible thing, so she could be on the road and clear of town before the rain hit, but she figured she had at least a few minutes left. She should accomplish something more than pie on her field trip.

There were at least four tourist-trap gift shops within the shopping district of "downtown," but the general store usually had the same stuff at a better price. Parking in front of the old-timey storefront, Mindy had to angle between two pickups—one a dually, one extended-cab with a roll bar. Pulling back out would be an exercise in blind faith. Two horses were hitched to the "Cowboy Parking Only" post. If Hilltop had been a bit closer to town, and if she wasn't so out of practice that her inner thighs still ached today, she might have been tempted to ride and avoid the hair-raising experiencing of weaving her small car between all the giant trucks. Too late now, though.

The place was empty, except for a clerk she didn't recognize. After they shared a polite smile and nod, Mindy passed by the T-shirts, the heavily tooled leather purses and horseshoe plaques with corny sayings on them, the racks of folksy candy in colorful packs, and made for a display of refrigerator magnets. Her cubicle mate at work collected them, and would probably love a new one. The cheesier the better.

Mindy was debating between the cowboy hat ("Bolero, TX— Cowboy Central!") and the pair of spurred boots ("Save a horse, ride a cowboy!") when the bells on the door announced a new customer had arrived.

The law.

Crisp, white straw hat. Khaki shirt with epaulets and insignia, dark olive pants. He even had the mirrored sunglasses, though he took them off a few seconds after entering the store, tucking one earpiece into his front shirt pocket to hold them as he nodded at the clerk.

"Bernie."

"Chet."

"How goes the battle this afternoon?" Chet's words were directed at the clerk but he was scanning the store, and as Bernie mumbled an answer, Chet's eyes lingered a fraction longer on Mindy than she was comfortable with.

She thought he frowned at her, but it was hard to tell through his dense mustache. It could have just been squinting as his eyes adjusted to being indoors. It made her feel vaguely guilty, anyway, suddenly terrified he would interpret her loitering over the magnets as a prelude to sticking one in her purse.

Logan's cousin Chet. He was a few years older, so she'd never gone to school with him. But in a town of under a thousand people, there was no escaping some level of acquaintance. She remembered him to look at, and she recalled the stories. Now he was the law, but there was a time when Chet Garcia had been the bane of the authorities in Bandera. Not because he was a bad kid, but because he was an infuriatingly good kid who did things like get up at town council meetings and argue about whether it was constitutional to have an age-based curfew. Or whether the wording of a particular ordinance against litter was unenforceable due to a grammatical error.

He'd been the captain of the debate team *and* the football team. And he'd also once used fireworks to blow up a cactus a hundred feet outside the city limits. Nobody was injured, and it hadn't been technically illegal, so the police held him for a few hours but ultimately had to let him go. The next week he'd posted an op-ed in the local paper about weaknesses in the city and county ordinances that had allowed for the legality of a potentially lethal explosive being detonated so near human habitations with no legal consequences. The following month, the city and county had pushed through additional regulations about explosives and noise nuisances. Mindy couldn't decide whether Chet's current position as sheriff was the ultimate irony or made the most sense of anything she'd ever heard.

Either way, he could definitely work the uniform. "Texas cop," right out of central casting. Late thirties, slightly stocky, mustachioed cowboy-turned-enforcer. Dark hair, with piercing gray eyes that were slightly startling against his sun-bronzed skin.

He's one of us.

Definitely hiding a freaky streak under that fine, upstanding exterior.

Chet turned down the store's central aisle and headed directly for the Slim Jims and jerky, grabbing several preserved meat items and returning to the counter to off-load them. The clerk started ringing them up while Chet backtracked for a large coffee. No cream, no sugar, just pure bitterness straight out of the dispenser into the biggest Styrofoam cup available.

Mindy realized she was staring about the time Chet finished paying and turned to leave. He stopped mid-pivot, meeting her gaze with curiosity then advancing toward her with purpose. Flustered, she dropped one of the magnets, then fumbled with the other, attempting to put it back on the metal display board.

"Mindy Valek?"

She'd been the homecoming queen, for fuck's sake. There was a time she could have *owned* this town if she'd wanted to. And she'd come here to do a job, not to perpetrate crimes; there was absolutely no need for her to be shaking in her boots next to a shelf full of plush armadillos in "Bolero" T-shirts. Besides, if she knew nothing else, she knew how to charm a random person into thinking she had her shit together. She pulled herself up, squaring her shoulders and unloading her biggest polite-society grin at him. "Chet Garcia. Well, look at you."

He didn't smile back. "Your left brake light is flickering."

"I beg your pardon?"

"Your left brake light," he repeated with a more obvious frown, "is *flickering*. And significantly dimmer than the right. If you'd been driving through town in bright sunlight when I saw your vehicle, I might have had to ticket you. However, as it's overcast, I was able to make out the light clearly and did not feel I could reasonably argue it was too dim to pass inspection. I *could* have written you a warning, but I dislike writing warnings for infractions people ought to be aware of on their own."

She tried to wrap her mind around all the words that had just come out of his somber mouth. She wasn't sure what she'd expected, but none of that had been it. "You mean a fix-it ticket?"

Chet grimaced. "Yes. A *fix-it* ticket. I dislike them."

"Okay." Nonplussed, she tried to figure out how to extricate herself from the conversation. "Thank you? I'll get somebody to look at it as soon as possible."

"Good." His expression shifted, looking more irked than anything else. He tapped one booted toe a few times, then sighed as if he'd made a decision he wasn't that happy with. "I *could* write you a ticket if I see the defective brake light again. As long as you're here in town that remains a possibility. Here in the vicinity. Within my jurisdiction. Which includes Hilltop Ranch."

Heat rose in Mindy's chest, and she clenched her hands into fists, then forced herself to relax. Checked that her smile was still in place as she asked a question she couldn't quite believe she was asking. "Are you . . . *threatening* me?"

He could've. Small Texas town, a sheriff drunk on power. Wouldn't be the first or last time that had happened. But Chet's face only grew more irritated. "No. That would be illegal." He sounded downright grumpy about that. But resigned. It was some comfort, at least.

"You were always a stickler for the law, weren't you?" It was true. Even his youthful rebellions had been about demonstrating where laws needed *improvement*.

"As a great man once said, 'You have to accept the rule of law, even when it's inconvenient, if you're going to be a country that abides by the rule of law.'"

"Benjamin Franklin, right?" It was a shot in the dark, but Mindy had long since discovered that most political quotes could be traced to about three people, and Benjamin Franklin was tops on the list.

Chet snorted, and his eyes suddenly sparkled in the fluorescent glare of the store. "Jesse Ventura."

She'd been punked, and it didn't feel good, so she pushed back. "The pet detective?"

The sparkle fizzled out as the glare returned. "The former professional wrestler turned Minnesota governor."

"Ah, I see." And she did. Chet was beating around the bush, but he knew why Mindy was there and he wanted her gone. And suddenly she was sick of subtext. "I have every right to be here. I have every right to be at your cousin's ranch. I didn't invent the oil and gas industry, and I'm really just trying to keep my job. Logan seems to have come to terms with my staying the week as a paying customer. If he wanted me gone . . ." If he wanted her gone, he probably wouldn't have strongly implied he was still planning to whip her and bang her before the week was out. "He's a big boy, he can fight his own battles. I know you helped finance the buyout so you're an interested party, but that's not really my problem. And it's not cool for you to be throwing your weight around at me when I'm innocently trying to pick out a refrigerator magnet for a friend."

At the "throwing your weight around," Chet moved a hand to his stomach, patting the khaki that stretched almost taut there. Some of the wind seemed to fall out of his sails. Mindy hadn't meant to hit a sore spot, but she couldn't bring herself to regret her words. Even if she had already decided to leave, she refused to be *pushed* out. And Chet rebounded quickly enough.

"These days, the law frowns upon running interlopers out of town on rails. Tarring and feathering are also off the table. This means my options, assuming you obey the letter of the law during your stay here, are limited to meaningful glares and the occasional heavy sigh."

"You could also shake your head in disappointment."

Thunder rumbled, and they both glanced toward the door for a second, then returned to the pissing contest.

"Don't think I won't resort to that if it's called for. But rest assured, if I issue you a ticket regarding the brake light it will only be to address a traffic safety issue. Enjoy your stay, Miss Valek." He tipped his hat.

She nodded, gracious in her dubious victory. "Thank you, Sheriff Garcia."

In the end, unable to decide, she bought both magnets. Also, because she liked the color and nothing more, a blue burnout T-shirt with "Bolero, Texas" in distressed Wanted-poster lettering inside a lasso graphic.

"My mom might like it." she explained to Bernie the clerk for no particular reason. "She's from here."

"Mm-hmm." Bernie swiped her card, then gave her the receipt to sign as he dumped everything in a plastic bag. Never cracked a smile.

So much for Texas hospitality.

Mindy grabbed the bag, stalked out the door . . . and watched the first fat drops of rain spatter onto the street beyond the awning.

Chapter Nine

Nobody had gotten shot. That was a definite plus. Maybe it was a low bar to set for his first hunting excursion at the ranch, but Logan was happy enough to have crossed it. Just a rabbit hunt, because nothing else but hogs and turkeys were in season, and there didn't seem to be any turkeys around lately. He hadn't wanted to start with a night hunt, and you needed that for hogs.

To be honest, no people *or rabbits* had been harmed on the trip. But the guests seemed happy enough. None of the four who'd gone hunting minded not bagging any rabbits. Mary Havlicek had gotten closest, and Logan had feared some grumbling about that from the three middle-aged men she'd sort of bested. But they'd all kept things in good spirits. Even raised a round of beer to Mary at the early brisket dinner Robert had laid out for them when they got back to the main compound.

The old house was darkening already by five, guests and staff alike concerned over the increasingly frequent severe weather warnings. Robert and Logan distributed bags of fruit, energy bars, and water bottles, so nobody would have to venture back out after dinner for snacks. Everybody's phones kept bleeping with emergency system signals, interrupting the meal. The laughter about it grew more and more tense as the barometer fell, and the first few heavy *plink*s of rain on the back porch's tin roof were enough to end the gathering.

Logan handed out umbrellas at the door, grateful his grandmother had always insisted on having enough to pass out to all the guests, and also glad that none of them seemed to be harboring any spiders.

"Please watch your step. Keep to the hard path. If you encounter any unexpected runoff, just come back to the house here and we'll put you up for the night."

Robert was the last one out the door. "Sorry, boss, but I'm actually out of here. I need to get back to my place before this gets too bad and make sure my cats aren't shitting on the bed. You gonna be okay on your own if anything happens?" He pushed away the umbrella Logan shoved at him, shaking his head with a smile.

Logan shrugged and slipped the umbrella back into the ceramic stand. "I'll be fine. I'll be inside where it's dry. I'll probably even have power and Wi-Fi unless this shit gets entirely too real."

Checking the blackening sky, Robert shook his head. "Optimists. I give your Wi-Fi about fifteen more minutes. Sir!" With a whoop and a grin, he hurtled off the front porch and down the rainy path toward the parking lot.

Only once Logan had closed the door did he realize he hadn't accounted for everyone.

Shit. Mindy was still out in the rain. Lamar said she'd gone to town for pie—was that a euphemism?—but she should have made it back for dinner.

Lightning flashed, still distant enough that the thunder came many seconds later.

Logan scanned his phone out of habit, looking for a text, before realizing she didn't have his private number. If she'd called the ranch line, there might be a voice mail patched through, but there didn't seem to be any of those, either. Not that she'd have had a reason to check in, of course. He had no cause to expect that. He shouldn't *want* to expect that.

But the rain had started to sweep down.

Possibly she was in her cabin, safe and sound. Logan punched in a quick text to Robert, asking him to swing by and check on his way to the car. He was already wet; the tiny detour wouldn't make him much wetter.

The wind picked up, and an ominous clattering, slapping sound sent a sliver of dread straight to Logan's heart.

"The fucking shutters!" he yelled aloud to the empty hall. "Fuck, fuck, *fuck!*"

The main house at the ranch was kind of a folly, a Victorian farmhouse that had been updated and added to over the years. His grandmother's addition had been shutters on the front and side windows—decorative ones on the top story, but real latching shutters on the bottom.

Logan sprinted to the window in the front parlor and shoved it open, reached for one of the shutters, then cursed himself and closed the sash again. He knew better, he'd done this chore enough times as a kid. There was no hope for it; he'd have to go out into the rain and secure all the shutters. And he needed to do it *now*, before the heaviest part of the storm hit.

His phone buzzed in his pocket and he yanked it out to check the text on the screen. Robert reported no sign of Mindy at the cabin.

Great. Flapping shutters and a lost guest. Superb start to his hospitality career.

He grabbed his hat off the rack by the front door as he dashed out of the house. He ignored the umbrellas—he'd need both hands, and the wind was picking up anyway so umbrellas would be useless soon.

It was dark as night now, only the faintest hint of greenish-purple illumination in the clouds. The color of tornados. He clamped down on that knowledge hard, because the forecast had only called for severe thunderstorms and there wasn't an active tornado watch *yet*.

The shutters along the front porch were covered. He decided to save those for last, and ducked around one side of the big, rambling house to catch the most exposed windows first. It was easy to spot the shutter that had come unhooked from its usual open position and was smacking the siding as the wind began to howl. Logan secured that one firmly closed, hoping the latch would hold through the storm so the shutter could protect the dining room window. The next two pairs were cooperative, but the last one had a slightly rusted hook that he finally gave up on. The mudroom window would just have to take its chances.

He was halfway down the other side of the house when his phone buzzed again. Drenched, not wanting to stop and take the damn thing out in the downpour, he ignored it and smacked another hook loose from its eyebolt, swinging the shutter shut and latching it securely. Two more shutters here and he was home free. Neither of them gave him any trouble.

Rounding the corner to return to the front porch, he saw a ghostly figure looming through the rain, and gasped before he could help himself.

Then he shook the rain from his eyes, the ghost ran a few steps closer, and he realized it was Mindy. Looking like a heroine from a scary movie, frankly. Pale as impending death, eyes dark with smeared makeup, soaked hair slicked back with rain. Her white but-ton-up shirt was practically see-through, but there was nothing very sexy about it.

"Jesus, Mindy, you scared the ever-lovin' crap outta me!" And relieved him so much it was all he could do not to scoop her into his arms.

"Sorry!" She dashed onto the porch ahead of him, then stared when he didn't follow her toward the door. "What the hell are you doing out here? Are you insane?"

He hit another rusted hook, this time nicking his hand in the effort to knock it loose. "No, I'm—*fuck*—trying to close the damn shutters. A little help would be nice."

After a second she jogged to the far end of the porch and started there, closing two shutters securely by the time he'd finally worked the stubborn hook loose. He caught up, finishing in time to meet her back in the middle and hold the front door open for her with a gesture that was as gallant as it was ironic.

"After you, ma'am." He swept his hat off with his free hand, and water splashed from the brim and crown to the porch.

Mindy nodded, looking like she was trying not to laugh as she preceded him into the house. "Thanks."

"Wait here." He shut and latched the door behind them. "I'll get you a towel. What are you doing here? When Robert said you weren't in your cabin I thought maybe you'd . . . Well, I don't know what I thought."

She shrugged and flipped her hair over her shoulder, wringing some drops from the ends onto the worse-for-wear entryway rug. "I don't know. I guess I just figured it would be rude to leave without saying anything. Then the rain started, and there was no time, so—"

"Wait, wait. What?" Her words were like brakes, squealing in his brain. Every rational thought process slammed to a halt.

"—I'm probably stuck for the night. I should've just gone straight to my cabin, but—"

"*Mindy.*"

"*Logan.* Hey, how about that towel?" She flipped her hair back again, brushed at her sodden shirt, stubbornly refusing to make eye contact. As he hesitated, debating whether to question her further, a shattering flash of lightning lit the place like daylight through the front door window, and even as both of them jumped, a crash of way-too-close thunder rattled the house.

Something was up. But keeping Mindy wet and dripping on the doormat wasn't going to help anything. Logan toed his boots off and slopped to the laundry room for two towels, pulling out his phone to check the texts he'd missed while outside wrangling the shutters. One was from Robert—he'd passed Mindy's car on his way out of the parking lot. The other was from his cousin Chet.

Encountered Mindy Valek. Flickering taillight. Pecan pie and coffee @ Minnie's. Souvenir magnets. Well-proportioned posterior.

Ah, Chet. Logan rubbed his hair with one towel as he brought the other back to a now-shivering Mindy. "You should come on in, I guess. Have you had dinner? Or just the pie?"

"Jesus, this town." She blotted the ends of her hair, then wrapped the towel over her shoulders as she leaned on the wall for balance while she got her boots off.

"Yeah. That why you're leaving?" *Without saying a word, if the storm had let you get away with it.* At this point Logan no longer knew how he should or shouldn't feel about that—he had no idea what they owed one another. No clear idea what he even wanted from Mindy; he only knew he *wanted* and wasn't going to *have.* He was just nice enough to know that the sense of disappointed entitlement made him a jerk, but that didn't cancel out the frustration.

Her shoulders slumped, her expression went blank. "I was always leaving anyway. I should never have come. Staying at all was the crazy decision, right? Leaving makes sense." She finally got enough leverage with her toe to shove her wet boot off. It landed on the floorboards with a sodden *thud.* "All kinds of sense."

Logan gave up pretending the towel would help his shirt get any drier, and started to unbutton it, heading back down the hall toward the kitchen and laundry room. "Especially after yesterday. Okay, fine. And then the storm really fucked with your plan, I guess. That must've sucked." He pulled the shirt off, transferring his sudden, ridiculous anger into jerky movements that made the task harder than necessary. "Shoulda checked the weather report a bit more closely."

An uneven *clomp*ing sound behind him told him she was following. He glanced back. She was still struggling to get her other boot off, stopping every few steps to make another attempt.

He snorted. *Fuck it. Let her figure it out on her own.* Then he smacked himself upside the head and stopped, pointing into the mudroom where the washer and dryer stood. "There's a bootjack by the back-back door there."

"The back-back door?" She peered into the room.

He flipped the light on and pointed again. "There. It's the back-back door because the kitchen door is the back door. Folks used to come in through the kitchen, and my grandmother got sick of it, so when she had the big washers and dryers put in, she insisted on a mudroom for that. So everybody could come in the *back*-back door and leave their shitkickers on the screen porch off the mudroom. Her wise contribution to the folly." He watched as Mindy made quick use of the old cast-iron bootjack, then dutifully turned the light back off after she was finished.

"I'll just put this up front with the other one." She vanished down the hall, and Logan leaned against the doorjamb separating the kitchen and the mudroom, giving himself a moment to breathe.

Robert had left a load of sheets or something tumbling in the dryer. The sweet smell of fabric softener and the rhythmic, familiar sound calmed Logan's nerves a small amount. Not quite enough to compensate for the sudden shock of Mindy's news. The problem wasn't her wanting to leave, so much. It was his instant rejection of the idea. His whole being had yelled such a firm *Nope* that he was still shaking it off.

But as Mindy had said, the crazy decision had been for her to stay once it was clear he wasn't interested in leasing the mineral rights. And, Logan reminded himself, he was *angry* at her for her deception. He should be *glad* she wanted to leave.

But sex, his lizard brain pointed out. *Compatible kinks. Lock that shit down.*

He wanted to lock it down. He wanted to lock that down *all night long*. Maybe even literally. She was stuck here in the storm anyway, couldn't possibly make the drive back to Dallas safely until tomorrow. She had named the giant spider in her cabin Moose. And she looked like a sunset until she smiled, and that was pure sunrise. *Dammit.*

He heard her footsteps in the hall and straightened up, then smiled at the sight of her coming through the kitchen doorway with her hair wrapped up in the towel. Her eyes flicked to his bare chest and he couldn't resist the tiniest pec flex.

"Could I get another towel? And do you mind pointing me to a restroom? I have another shirt I can change into . . ."

She held up a plastic shopping bag he hadn't noticed her holding before. More than souvenir magnets, it looked like. "Uh, sure. It's back down the hall, under the stairs. Would you rather just have a robe?"

He leaned back into the laundry room, reached for one of the high shelves by the door, and pulled down a robe—a thick, creamy, monogrammed prototype, still wrapped in plastic with a wide grosgrain ribbon tied around the bundle. His grandparents had always offered them for sale to guests; Logan was still deciding whether it was worth it, but he was glad he had a sample to hand Mindy in her hour of need.

She eyed the packaged robe, then him. "I should really just grab some food and head back to my cabin." Another thunderclap nearly drowned out her words.

"Not until this dies down. I can just see the headlines. 'Tragedy Strikes at Hilltop.' 'Local Homecoming Queen Meets Shocking End.' 'Area Man's Dude Ranch Dream Struck Down by Lightning.'"

"Those are not good headlines."

"I *know*."

"I mean, they're not well constructed for—oh, fine, just give me the robe."

Then she *smiled*. Dammit.

He started to hand her the robe, but held on to it. "I don't want you to leave."

She tugged at the plastic. "I won't walk back in the thunderstorm. You're right, that's not—"

"No, I mean *early*. I don't want you to leave *early*. I want you to stay. Not just because of the rain." Not just for sex, but he wasn't willing to examine that part too closely yet. He certainly wasn't willing to discuss it. But it had to be Mindy's decision, anyway. All he could do was put it out there. This . . . very slightly open emotional door. He could just point out that it was there and it was open and she was welcome to come in for a visit.

Or something.

Her fingers curled around the pale blue ribbon. She tugged harder, finally freeing the robe from his hands. The smile was gone. "Look, I'm having a lot of fun with you, okay? I'm enjoying your company." She held the robe against her chest like armor.

Logan squinted, trying to read her expression and failing utterly. Her mouth said "*fun*" and "*enjoy*," but her face and body said "*miserable*," and he couldn't figure it out. "I'm having fun, too. We're enjoying each other."

"And that's exactly why I can't stay."

She lingered in the powder room as long as possible, probably longer than was reasonable. After she used the restroom, washed her hands, stripped off her clothes, and toweled herself dry, she bundled into the robe and sat down to think and avoid facing Logan again. She knew eventually he'd come knocking, and that she shouldn't wait long enough for that to happen. But he gave her more time than she expected.

She heard his footsteps, heavy on the stairs over her head, while she was changing. He came back down a few minutes later, thumping unevenly like he was taking the steps a few at a time. Still a gangly, dorky teenager inside. Of course, she was no better.

Washing her hands a second time bought her a few seconds more. She tested some of the vanilla-scented hand lotion from the brass-topped pump dispenser on the marble vanity. Admired the dark red flocked wallpaper—it looked delightfully like something from an old-timey bordello, which she suspected was the goal. Studied the three delicately tinted old photographs of ladies with Gibson girl updos and bee-stung lips.

Either Logan's grandma had decorated this room, or *somebody's* grandmother had, and it was perfect. If she could just stay in this tiny, carefully curated space, nothing bad could ever befall her, and she would never have to face life on the other side of the door again.

Her stomach growled loudly, reminding her this plan had flaws. Stress always made her hungry, and she'd gone light on lunch in anticipation of pie.

Cursing softly at herself, she scooped up her wet clothes in the damp towel, placed her hand on the crystal doorknob, and steeled herself for the confrontation.

She opened the door to an empty hallway and the sound of swelling violins. She followed it to the kitchen, where Logan was humming along to the classical music and putting food on a plate, complete with hand flourishes in time with the music after he placed each item. He'd changed into plaid flannel lounge pants that hung on his hips in an almost painfully flattering way.

"*Ba-dum-dum-dum!*" He flipped a piece of brisket onto the china and then pulled the fork away, waving it in the air as if conducting an invisible orchestra while the music swooped into a particularly romantic passage. Outside, the sky flickered and boomed in perfect natural counterpoint. A branch was blown along the shuttered kitchen window just as the violins skittered into moody disorder. Logan had chosen the perfect soundtrack for the storm. It thundered again, and he echoed with a sound-effect *boom-crash* noise, twirling his fork to bring the flutes into play as the lightning flashed.

Finally she cleared her throat. "Nice music."

Logan jumped back from the counter, whirling around. "Mindy!"

Were they doing that again? "Logan."

He grinned, dragging his gaze slowly down to her toes then back up, as if the fluffy robe was the hottest outfit he'd ever seen. Then he waggled his eyebrows. "Mindy . . ."

She held her hands up in the universal back-off gesture, punctuating it with a stern glare. "Logan."

"Fair enough. Uh, I put together some of the brisket and potatoes, broccoli. Sorry, no cheese sauce left." He brought the plate and utensils to the island and set it down with another flourish, not quite as grand as his earlier display. "I figured you could eat while we talk."

Her stomach gurgled at the sight of the food. There was no use resisting; she made for the stool and picked up the fork. "Okay. So I wouldn't have pegged you for a classical music guy."

He sucked air through his teeth, studying the lamp for a second. "I guess this would be a bad time to make a joke about how you wouldn't have pegged me at all."

"You just *made* the joke, though." She sliced a piece of brisket.

"Right, right."

"Wasn't that funny."

The first bite of meat melted in her mouth. It was *heaven*. That rarest of all things, a tender brisket. She had to concentrate to make sense of Logan's response.

"You're just hangry. So the music is, uh . . . what my granddad always used to play out here when the weather got bad. He had an LP. Probably still in the bookcase in the front parlor, come to think of it. It's Mendelssohn's *Hebrides Overture*. He thought it sounded like a thunderstorm rolling in."

She nodded, too involved in the brisket to express any further surprise. The bathroom had been good, but this was better, this warmly lit kitchen with a plate full of delicious food.

Served to her by a handsome, problematic man she couldn't let herself fall for.

Tracking her fork through the mashed potatoes, she considered a moment, framing her words. She had made a decision. She ought to stick to it. "So here's my problem. I thought it could just be a few scenes. You know? We'd do that while I was here, it would be a kinky vacation, we'd both get some stress relief. No harm, no foul, no hard feelings about why I came here in the first place. *But.* I need to leave because I'm having as much fun building fire pits and listening to you talk about your grandfather's rain music as I am getting my ass switched and rubbing off on you in the spider shack. Obviously you're not somebody I can be involved with. For many reasons. But mostly conflict of interest, plus history and geography. And I feel like I'm really crossing the streams, here, in ways I normally am very careful to avoid." She exhaled hard and finally took the bite, studying her plate to give Logan a chance to think about his response.

"So," he started. Then he breathed out hard, echoing her, and took a long pause before trying again. "So my first instinct is to tell you, my dick's not that magic. If you're worried you'll be drawn into my thrall if we actually fuck, and therefore be unable to leave when the week is up, I can reassure you that hasn't been my experience with women in the past. I mean, I do *okay*." He shrugged, then grabbed his crotch through his flannel pants like he was reassuring himself. "I do *just fine*. I've had no complaints. There's nothing wrong with it, it's an okay size, disease-free, I'm fairly confident I know what to do with it. I'm just saying, it doesn't emit magic spooge or anything."

"I've met it," she reminded him, once she'd managed to swallow the potatoes without snort-laughing them out her nose. "Fairly recently, too. I'm surprised you don't remember."

"Just saying."

She put a hand on his arm and gave him an earnest pat. "I wasn't concerned about becoming enthralled by your magic spooge."

"Well, that's a relief." He scooped a dab of potato up with his index finger and ate it, so quickly she almost missed it. "If that's not a danger, then, what is it?"

The guy who makes me laugh about magic spunk, and the circus horse he rode in on. "You're a weird Dom."

"I'm an awesome Dom. Answer the question, Melinda." He brought the Dom voice into play, dropped into it just like that. Shot her the Blue Steel look and everything. Lethal. Did he have a license to concealed-carry that weapon?

She decided to go for something like honesty. Not the whole truth, but a big part of it. "It's this place. Not the ranch, the town. Being back here's just . . . It's stirred up a lot of shit for me. And I don't want to wallow in that. That's not me." That part was the lie. Because this *was* her, this diner-pie girl, this woman who'd kept those broken-in boots in the back of the closet for so many years. The dust from this place was in her blood. Even taciturn Bernie at the general store had sounded *right* to her ears. So she told another partial truth. "I'm homesick." And if she stayed in Bolero, if she gave in to the homesickness that wanted to keep her here, she'd lose the life she'd spent so much time and energy and passion building.

Logan sounded right, felt right. Smelled and tasted right. But only because—she insisted to herself—he was the focal point for this wave of nostalgia. The living embodiment of Bolero, with kink on top as an added enticement. And it *was* enticing. So much so she could barely breathe when they made eye contact for any length of time. But that would fade once she got back to Dallas, saw her friends, hit the club, went back to the office.

He nodded, the stern face thawing into friendly sympathy. "And I've been kind of an asshole to you." He returned the friendly pat, his big hand warming her arm through the robe. As he leaned in, she could still smell the rain on him. His bare chest took up her whole field of view. "You know, what with literally beating you and all."

"So, are we even, then? For my sneaking around at the beginning?" She hoped it sounded light and casual, but she doubted it. Honestly, she wondered how she was even coherent. He'd left his hand on her arm instead of taking it away after the condescending gesture, and her heart had started to pound, and now her face and pussy were both buzzing with heat, and she was screwed, she was just absolutely screwed.

Logan slid his hand down to hers, smoothed his fingers around to her palm, and teased open her clenched fist so he could lace their fingers together. "I'd say we're *nearly* even, sure. A little extra reinforcement couldn't hurt, but I want to leave that up to you. So I can make up one of the spare beds—which, I'll warn you, won't be that comfortable, I still need to replace some mattresses—or the couch in the office, which is probably a better bet. Or we can get freaky for a while, and then if you want, you can sleep with me. Any combination of those things would be fine."

She swallowed hard. It was one night. They'd already done so much—surely a little more wouldn't make that much difference. It wouldn't be any harder to walk away if she allowed herself one more round of playtime, and one night of whatever followed that. "I'm out of here tomorrow, though."

"Understood. No strings. Just playing and sex. And sleeping."

"Okay, then."

"Okay?" He sounded brashly eager for a second, then seemed to recall himself. "I think you meant, 'Please, sir, may I have a scene that isn't just seventy percent blowies and frottage in the spider shack.'"

She giggled, glancing up at him. He'd smoothed his demeanor and was keeping it utterly deadpan. Dom skills, indeed. She needed to get on his level. "Please, sir, may I have a scene that isn't just seventy percent blowies and frottage in the spider shack."

"You *may*." He nudged her plate a half inch closer to her. "So eat up. You're gonna need your strength."

Chapter Ten

He made Mindy wait an hour after eating. He wasn't that subtle about checking the time while they talked—on the nearest clock, on his phone—and finally she called him on it.

"You have somewhere else you need to be?"

"Nope."

"Are you making me wait an hour before I go in swimming?"

"Yep."

"Well, okay then. *Sir*."

"When you said that, it sounded like . . . *Ladies*."

Mindy chuckled and wrapped the robe more snugly under her feet. She was tucked into the corner of the couch in the office, wedged between the arm of the couch and a big throw pillow with a needle-point sunset on it, and cuddled down into the oversized robe as though the raging thunderstorm outside had actually made it colder inside, instead of just more humid.

She smirked. "*Gentlemen*."

"Makes everything dirtier." He turned back to his computer screen and pretended to continue casually checking his email. As if he wasn't pressing the heel of his non-mousing hand against his thigh to keep his leg from tapping.

Behind him, Mindy stretched and sighed. The breathy sound was way too close to a sex noise. He figured she was doing it accidentally-on-purpose, but he was 100 percent okay with that.

The text in front of him swam. He couldn't process anything but the mental checklist of what he had available to him up in his bedroom. His toy bag was in the closet, but most of his equipment was in secret storage in Houston. He'd told everyone he'd completely committed to the plan to restore Hilltop to its former glory. But that hadn't kept him from maintaining an escape route. All his furniture, the few pieces of artwork he'd collected over the years, and the vast majority of his kink arsenal were all safely stored in a climate-controlled space near his old house.

He really could have used the hour to catch up on work. He was still building an inventory database for the ranch, and he had a list of point-of-sale systems to compare so Hilltop could start selling things like monogrammed robes and caps with logos and T-shirts and art from local artists. He also needed to research whether or not he could get a liquor license. So many things tugging his mind in different directions. So many concerns, more every day, about whether he could even make Hilltop viable again. But the strongest pull was right behind him; Mindy's attention was a steady but gentle undertow in the current of information.

She'd already figured out his plan, so when the hour clicked over he gave up any pretense of trying to finish the inventory form he was tweaking, and swiveled his chair around to face her. Crossed his arms over his chest, put his Dom face on.

Mindy bit her lip and raised her eyebrows at him, then lowered her gaze to her lap. "Tick-tick-tick-tick-*ding!*"

He snorted, then kicked himself for it as he schooled his features back into sternness. Mindy wasn't a brat *exactly*, but she wasn't all that into roles. Usually he wasn't, either, especially once he got to know somebody, but he'd intended to keep some distance tonight. Pretend it was a club scene with a relative stranger, with everyone on their best behavior.

Brisk. Businesslike. A transaction where everybody was up-front and got their needs met. That's what was called for here.

"Let's have the talk. Safe words?"

She glanced up then back down again. "Red for stop, yellow for slow down."

"Clarify what you mean, with yellow."

"Oh, well . . ." Playing with the ends of the robe's sash, she pondered for a few seconds before answering with more hesitation than he'd expected. "Yellow means I want you to . . . pull back on whatever you're doing and check in with me. So just give me a minute to decide if I want . . . if I can keep going or not? And talk it over. If that works for you?"

Frowning, he unfolded his arms and rolled his chair closer to the couch. "Why wouldn't it work for me?"

She shrugged, flipping one of the sash ends back and forth over her wrist. Lashing herself with it very gently, Logan realized.

"Some Doms are kind of dicks about that," she said with another shrug. "They don't want a discussion, it's just a chance to talk you into doing what they want. Spare me from people who see safe words as a challenge, you know? I assume you aren't one of them, but I've made that assumption before and been wrong."

"Jesus. A safe word is a safe word. Hey." He leaned in, touching her knee gently until she looked up. "There are things I'm a dick about, but that isn't one of them. If my partner isn't into it, I don't want to keep doing it. So obviously we stop and work that shit out." He sort of wanted to ask who the fuck she'd been playing with in Dallas, but he knew it was none of his business. And he knew that the same things happened all over. People could be horrible; it wasn't news. It wasn't unique to kink, either. Dating was a bitch. He sat back and tried to resume his Dom pose. "As a baseline, let's assume we're both going to try not to be assholes to each other, all right? And that consent is always the hottest thing."

She smiled enough to invoke a dimple on one side. "I've never been more attracted to you than right now. But at the same time I just realized how low I'm setting my bar? I'm getting it up for basic human decency. I don't want you to think my standards aren't higher than that."

His comfy lounge pants felt a size smaller all of a sudden. "You're getting what up, exactly? Can I see?"

Mindy giggled, and Logan's plan to keep things serious started to crumble around the edges. "We haven't finished having the important talk yet."

"We can talk with the robe open. Being naked doesn't keep your mouth from functioning."

She rolled her eyes. "Fiiiiine." But the way she slipped the knot and parted the thick terry cloth to reveal herself made it obvious she didn't have a problem with it. "I'm more concerned about how our brains will be functioning, but fine."

It was a fair point. He hadn't really expected her to do it, and the sudden sight of taut pink nipples and auburn bush made all the blood rush straight from Logan's brain to his cock. Not to mention all that skin—smooth, as-yet-unmarked thighs, a blank canvas. Then he started wondering about the back view, and whether she might not have at least a *few* marks there already. *His* marks. Her left breast bore a deep, reddening bruise below the nipple where he'd sunk his teeth into it the day before.

He needed several seconds to breathe before he could remember what they were supposed to be talking about.

Limits. Equipment. Sex. *Right.* "I don't have that many toys with me right now, but it's mostly impact stuff. I'll use either that or my bare hand." She gave him a thumbs-up, so he continued, trying to ignore how even that small movement made her breasts jiggle enticingly. "Any areas off-limits? Any injuries I should know about?"

"You can touch whatever you want. For impact, my face and my arms are out. I have mostly T-shirts with me, so nothing that'll leave marks that could show when I'm wearing a T-shirt."

"Is slapping okay, as long as it's not on the face?" He tried not to picture what it would feel like to slap the boob with the bruise on it, tried desperately not to imagine the noise she'd make.

Mindy squirmed, shifting her feet from under her. "Yeah. Fine. No humiliation, though, please." Her voice had gone higher, softer.

The scene hadn't officially started, but they were clearly in the warm-up. Logan propped one foot on the couch next to her legs. "Got it. Why don't you take that robe all the way off." Not an order. But not a question. He wanted to see what she would do with it.

She held up a finger. "Your front door is half glass, and the hall and stairway are in full view of that, where anybody at the door can see if I walk out of this room naked, so . . . no, I'll wait until we're upstairs, unless we're gonna be playing in here the whole time?"

Logan resisted a facepalm. He really *was* thinking with his little head. "Right, right. Sorry. We might start in here, but you can keep the robe on for now. Ah, okay. Restraints? Gag? Blindfold? Any hard limits there?"

"Restraints are great. No gagging, no hoods. No total sensory deprivation or anything that blocks my nose or mouth, but a blindfold . . . is fine." She quirked her lips and squirmed again. Logan made a mental note to get her blindfolded as soon as humanly possible. "No edge play tonight. Sharps, blood, fire, electro, breath play. None of that."

A double mention for breath play. It was clearly a rock-hard limit; the rest sounded more situational. The petroleum engineer in him wanted to start plotting all this information into a database, and mapping it onto charts. Figuring out the formulas, the variables, the tolerances. "Allergic to anything? Lube ingredients? Latex? *Crap*, I hope you aren't allergic to latex, I don't have any polypro . . ."

"Latex is fine. I don't think I have any allergies. One time I got a rash after this thing with capsaicin cream, but . . ." She shrugged. "Oh yeah, please don't use capsaicin cream."

"Wasn't planning on it." But now he was really curious about where that rash had been located. "Are we forgetting anything?"

Mindy studied the ceiling, poking her tongue into one cheek as she considered. "Uh, probably?"

He edged closer and lifted his other foot to the couch, bracketing her. Giving his balls and half-mast erection some breathing room, mostly, but also just asserting himself. "Do you have a scene name? Would you feel more comfortable with that?" He hoped she'd say no.

Mindy blushed—not a coy blush, a sheepish one. "It's . . . Ariel. You don't have to use it."

"*Ariel?* As in *The Little Mermaid?*" Another piece of his childhood destroyed, but in the best possible way.

"I didn't think it up myself," she said defensively. "Two of my kink friends started calling me that and it just stuck."

"I love it. But I won't use it if you don't want me to."

"Mindy's fine. Or . . . Melinda, if you want."

Logan flexed his thighs inward ever so slightly. "You like the scolding thing, don't you?"

She nodded, holding up a thumb and forefinger a half inch apart. "Little bit. Um, what about protocol? Do you want . . . Logan, or sir, or Master Something, or—uh, am I gonna have to do Gor poses or anything? I kind of suck at that vibe."

You think? He tried to picture her kneeling like a perfect submissive *kajira*, serving him tea or cleaning his shoes, and laughed out loud. "Not my jam, either." It was so *not her* that the idea didn't even really turn him on. Much.

"Phew. Okay, so . . . ?"

"'Sir' if you feel like it. If it's not working for you, don't force it."

"So I'll skip it," she suggested, "if it's gonna feel like '*Ladies*.' Good to know. That's refreshing."

It wasn't going to be a serious, businesslike scene. How had he ever thought it could be? But this could be more dangerous than expected, if they were friendly and informal with each other while they played. Because that dynamic was his favorite. More and more, Mindy was turning out to be a walking collection of his favorite things; he had to work to tell himself that didn't mean *she* was his favorite.

He caught her shifting her eyes, glancing at his legs on either side of her, a quick look between. She was edgier about the situation than she let on. And it was time to put her directly on edge and keep her there for as long as they could both stand it.

"Okay, then. Last question. What's your position on brinking?"

"Brinking? It can be hot, I guess?"

"Cool, cool. And you're good with waiting for permission to come?" When she nodded, he pulled himself as close to the couch as the chair would allow, and reached out to nudge Mindy's knee. She had scooted off her feet, but her legs were still folded up, her feet peeking out from under the robe to her side. "Open up."

"Oh, we're . . . we're starting?" She looked adorably confused for half a second.

Logan pushed the robe out of the way, slid his hand from her knee to her hip, and gave her a fast, hard swat. "Yes, we're starting." He put his hand on her knee again, pushing more firmly. "So open up."

She lifted her knee, spreading her thighs wide, giving him full access. Her leg trembled a little and he stifled an evil chuckle as he smoothed his hand down her inner thigh to the softest, plumpest part of it, inches from her pussy. When he squeezed there, the movement tugged her skin tight, pulled her pussy wider. Logan heard the soft, wet noise of her cunt lips spreading, just before Mindy breathed in sharply, masking the sound.

He pinched tighter, concentrating his effort on one spot until Mindy gave up a soft whimper. His cock responded to the noise. Mindy seemed to respond to the pain, as well, opening her leg still further and breathing faster.

Patience. Logan eased his grip, soothing the spot with a stroke of his fingers before trailing them down to Mindy's cunt. She was flushed, hot, and slick. So ready for his exploring fingers as he traced and spread the delicate folds then ringed her clit a few times with only enough pressure to tease.

When she started to relax into it, he pressed his thumb there more firmly, and used his other hand to attack the pinching spot again. "Don't move."

She trembled with the effort as the pain intensified, making a distressed noise in the back of her throat. He wasn't doing anything major yet, and she still seemed entirely present. No subspace to mess with her perceptions or ease her tension. No transition from warm-up to real pain. It just *hurt*, and she showed that, which made him hard—but he wanted to find out what it did for *her*.

After another few seconds he moved his thumb, drawing a slow, steady circle on her clit. Her face squeezed in, her brows drew together . . . then she exhaled slowly, shakily, forcing her shoulder down as the air left her. Processing the pain, figuring it out, reaching for the pleasure.

Her next sound was another soft cry, a rising note, almost like music. Really, almost like . . .

Ariel. Oh, fuck a duck. He bit his lip to keep from laughing. But after a second it was hotter than it was funny.

When he took his hands away, she stared after them avidly. Longingly. But aside from that, she didn't move a muscle.

A bloom of pink spread where he'd pinched her. It was nearly the same shade as her pussy lips. Nearly the same shade, when he looked up, as her mouth—which was starting to curve into a soft, dreamy smile.

Detached. Businesslike. Functional. Practical. *Bullshit.* Logan leaned in and kissed her.

Mindy tried to breathe, tried to sort through the sensations. The pain was sharper than she'd expected this soon, but sweeter, too. She'd been ready for a flogging, maybe a riding crop. All the touching was a pleasant shock. Hands were so personal.

Mouths, in a way, were even more so. They'd kissed before, but this felt new. Logan was turned on, she could see his erection in the loose pajama pants, but he kissed her like there was all the time in the world. Like it wasn't a question of overwhelming passion, but *intention.* Why that should be so hot, she had no idea, but it made her even wetter.

Being naked, even partially naked, felt almost *too* good. It had taken all her common sense and willpower not to yank the robe off earlier when he'd suggested it. Now it was a huge, unwieldy presence around her, hindering her from the exposure she craved. Common sense was leaving her. If he ordered the robe off now, she'd shed it in a heartbeat. In another few minutes, she suspected, he could order her to walk naked through the barnyard and she'd do it, thunderstorm and guests be damned.

She fisted the folds of the plush robe, working to stay still as he plundered her mouth. He'd told her not to move, and she was good at following orders. *So good at it.*

He drew back, nibbling at her lips, and she didn't even have to fight the urge to chase him down for another deeper kiss because she knew what her job was here. Not to move.

Her brain made room for that one idea, holding it, pushing everything else back. That single directive shone steady and bright, in a wide-open space ready for more orders to fill it. She'd been resisting this for days—in the barn, around the ranch, in the toolshed. Now the cumulative effect of all that forbearance came into play, hard. A little bit of pain, a little bit of privacy, the knowledge that tonight, nothing was stopping them . . . these were enough to undo her now.

Logan released her lips slowly. A puff of shared air, hot and sweet and redolent of brisket, washed her face. Then he raised a finger to her forehead and ran it down her nose, tracing her lips, pushing slightly inside her mouth. She flicked her tongue over his fingertip, tasting herself on him before he pulled the digit away and continued on his path over her chin and down to her throat.

He slid his hand around her neck and held it there, heavy and warm. Not constricting her throat, just laying claim. His face was thoughtful and stern and beautiful and angelic and she realized she was already falling into subspace a second before he spoke.

"Time to go upstairs."

"Mm-hmm."

His gaze shifted to her face and he smirked in a way only sadists knew. "You're already starting to fly, aren't you?"

She couldn't shrug—he'd told her not to move—so she smiled back. Because he really was the dreamiest thing. "Mmm. Sir."

"Oh, God. This is gonna be good." He stood, shoving the rolling chair back, and put his hands out. A clear enough directive. She took them and let him pull her up from the couch. He let her go once she was standing, and nodded down at her chest before heading toward the hall. "Tie that back up. You weren't wrong about the privacy concerns."

After a second of confusion, she realized he meant the robe. She fumbled for the loose ends of the sash, tugged the lapels tighter, and belted it back into place as she followed him out of the office. He stopped for a few seconds at the front door, looking out the window. There was still a lot of rain, some thunder and lightning, but nothing like an hour earlier.

He didn't comment on the weather. He turned and headed up the stairs, and Mindy floated after him.

Logan's bedroom was at one end of the long upstairs hallway, and under different circumstances Mindy might have stopped to look around and appreciate the restoration work once he'd flicked on the bedside lamp. Tonight all she cared about was the enormous brass bed, the blinds that looked adequate to block anybody's view, and the black duffel bag Logan pulled out of his closet.

He spared her a quick look while he was unzipping it. "Strip."

"Oh. Yes, sir." She dropped the robe and relaxed into the warm, humid air of the room. Naked was so good. Naked was almost always better.

"Here's what I have." Logan pulled things out of his toy bag, lining some of them up on the long, dark wood dresser, putting others back into the duffel. The winning objects included a lovely, heavy, well-conditioned flogger, a crop, two sets of leather cuffs with buckles, what looked like a collapsible spreader bar, a box of condoms, and a large bottle of lube. A few carabiners and some safety clips, and a pair of short horse leads that looked like they had been liberated from the tack room.

Certainly more than enough to be going on with.

She was losing a bit of her buzz, but she didn't mind. "I love looking in people's toy bags."

"I don't have much in here right now. So much stuff in storage. All my clamps and dildos, almost all of my whips and canes, my knives. A ton of rope. A big vibe." Logan pulled out a long, slender, transparent Lucite shaft, swishing it through the air into his palm in a practice stroke before laying it next to the other equipment. "It's actually a venetian blind rod. It might break, I don't know. But I wanted to try it out. It's new to me so if I use it, I'll go slow."

"M'kay." Canes were evil, but she could easily reach a point where she didn't mind the evil.

He shot her a look. "I've lost my 'sir.' We need to fix that."

She had been fine until he pointed it out. Suddenly there she was, naked and self-conscious in his bedroom, looking at the stuff he planned to beat her with, and the sheer insanity of it bubbled up as fast as a shaken soda bottle. He knew her parents. He'd been her math tutor. His kinky cousin the sheriff wanted to run her out of town. How could this be her life?

"Sorry. Sir. I don't know . . ." What to do with her *hands*. Where to *look*. What to *say*. What to *think*. She twisted her fingers together in front of her and eyed the robe on the floor. She could grab it, be out of here in an instant.

Logan stepped toward her and put his hands on her shoulder, pressing down, smoothing her knotted muscles. "Hey, now. Whoa. Easy. I didn't mean to bring you back up and strand you. C'mere."

She obeyed the pressure of his fingers, leaning into his chest, letting him enfold her and tip her chin up. His kiss was a fixed point of certainty, a port in a storm. And when he took her bottom lip between his teeth and bit down until she moaned, she felt as much relief as pain.

Her tongue was next, captured and tortured and released after a dazzling moment of too-sharp, sickening pain that made her squeal and pant. She didn't *like* having her tongue bitten, but it was effective. Like a jump-start for her stalled endorphins.

One of Logan's big, soothing hands found its gentle way to her breast, the one with the bite mark on it. He pinched the flesh there and kissed her sweetly and, when she whimpered, stroked his other hand down to her butt to press her closer. His erection was hard, pushy, pressing into her lower belly like a demand. She wanted him, almost more than she wanted the scene. But the scene was what they both needed.

He lifted her onto her toes, pushing a knee between her legs the way he had in the toolshed, and her urge to flee evaporated in a rush of renewed desire.

"Now, this is good," he murmured in her ear as he coaxed her into a familiar rhythm against his thigh. "This is how I would've liked you yesterday. Naked, and leaving a wet mess all over my pants when you rub off."

He gripped her ass, squeezing each time she thrust, digging his fingers deeper into the bruise he'd left by pinching her the day before. How did he know exactly where it was without even looking? Magic? Pain radiated from his touch, then heat, pure and vital.

She shifted her angle, bringing her clit more firmly against his warm, flannel-covered thigh. A mindless tempo, a simple goal. A weight lifted from her shoulders, her thoughts and body started to soar—

And Logan hoisted her back a step by her armpits, smirking again. "Better. Much better. Now we can get to the good stuff."

Chapter Eleven

It was always harder with somebody new. Feeling out boundaries, learning soft limits. Mindy had been there many times.

All the things that couldn't be stated. The things you only knew about yourself when somebody else discovered them—those elements were absent with a new partner. You only had what you'd told each other, and what you could pick up on the fly. And that was often fun, but sometimes it meant there wasn't any flow.

She needed the flow to get into subspace. She needed subspace to take more pain. She needed more pain—more *handling*—to get the most out of the scene. She hadn't expected any of that with Logan tonight. They'd basically just been flirting up to this point. From Mindy's perspective, this was really the first time. She'd counted on that detachment, that mild dissatisfaction. Counted on things not going perfectly. Because that would be easier to walk away from.

And yet . . . she knew Logan. They came from the same place, and had taken the same things away from it. And now they were both back here, for whatever reasons, feeling like they had unfinished business. When he directed her to stand by the bed, to hold out her hands for the cuffs, the choreography was as smooth as if they'd done this dance a thousand times.

He buckled the cuffs, checking carefully to make sure they weren't too tight, then clipped them together around one curved railing detail of the metal footboard—which wasn't brass, as Mindy had originally thought, but heavy wrought iron. When she tugged, it didn't budge at all. She knew the cuffs were fastened to the railing with safety clips that she could unhook at any time if she liked. But the illusion of being bound was so strong she struggled for a moment by instinct. Logan pressed on her shoulders again, making low noises in his throat as if he were gentling a fractious horse. Once she'd calmed, his hands drifted lower, exploring. Like magic, he left tingling awareness everywhere he touched, forging a path of shivering anticipation from her waist to her knees.

"Let's see . . . you still have a nice stripe here from the switch . . ." He raked a nail across her lower back from left to right, stinging the tender skin. "Close to the kidneys, I need to watch that. Sorry. And then *this* bruise." His thumb dug into the pinch mark, and Mindy winced at the deep, aching jab. Then he scratched over her butt with both hands, all the way down to her upper thighs. "And *two* pretty welts down here. Wow, I'd like to get you on a horse now and watch you trot all over this ranch. Or maybe I'll wait and do that after I've added a bit more."

He slapped each upper thigh, each cheek, a quick back-and-forth. Startling, not painful. Mindy giggled nervously, tried to cover her mouth with her hands, was hindered by the cuffs. The panic had left her, though. The restraint felt good. Necessary. She was anchored by the bed frame. Held together by the cuffs.

Logan moved behind her, selecting something from the array on the dresser. She expected a blow next, and was startled by the gentle, thick *flump* of leather flogger falls over her shoulder. She buried her nose in the leather for a second, overwhelmed by the smell as always.

"You like that?" Logan pressed up behind her, gathering her hair in one hand and tugging lightly.

"Mm-hmm. Smells good, sir." It smelled intoxicating. Probably because she was conditioned to know what it could do for her. But the reason didn't matter. The leather was butter-smooth and thick, possibly elk, beautifully worked. It looked and felt expensive.

Logan pulled her head back by his makeshift handle, stealing a quick kiss. "Next time you need to wear a ponytail or something." He smoothed the twisted hair to the front of her shoulder.

She nodded, not thinking about the "next time" until he'd already released her and backed away with the flogger. The first slap of the falls against her butt drove all thought out of her mind.

It was a good warm-up—mostly thud, a hint of sting, enough to set her skin humming and clear her head completely. Logan knew what he was doing, starting with a light rain of blows to her butt and shoulders, then working his way up and down as he increased the intensity. Hard, harder . . . then almost too hard, and both of them grunted at each blow, until he released a wallop against her upper thighs that made her yelp and flinch away.

"Two more like that," he said quietly. "Grab the bedpost. Stand still."

Breathing through the pain, Mindy fumbled her wrists around in the cuffs, wrapped her hands around the cold iron, and concentrated on holding still.

The next strike caught one of her upper thighs in a smacking burn, like being punched with a beehive. *Too much, too much.* But *too much* was her catnip. She dove into the pain, let it take her over, felt the rush and the pulse between her legs as it quickened along with her heartbeat.

Whack! On the other leg. The last one almost knocked her over, and she and Logan groaned in tandem with effort and effect. She could hear it in his voice, that it was good for him, too, and that filtered into the overall mix of how good it was for her.

Then he was behind her again, leaning in, his cock pressing against her butt, one arm circling her waist to support her. He kissed the top of her shoulder, the muscle leading from her neck to her arm, slowly working his way up to the tender spot behind her ear. His free hand roamed, first fondling one breast, then slipping down her belly to tease and tug at her pubic hair.

"Good warm-up," he muttered into her skin; his breath heated the whole side of her body from that sensitive point. "You make some really good noises." To prove how good, he ground against her, a slow press and release, press and release, just as he slid his fingers down to her clit.

Her body melted into unfettered lust, centered around the tip of Logan's finger. He stroked a small, steady circle there, and between his fingers, the lingering pain from the flogging, and the shiver-inducing attention to the secret-weapon spot on her neck, Mindy was close to orgasm within seconds. So close. She needed it.

"Yesssss," she whispered. Her hips moved despite her strict orders to them to stay still.

"Tell me when you're almost there." Logan increased his pressure a fraction, bit lightly on her neck.

"Oh God . . ." And then she remembered. *Brinking.* Fuck. "I'm gonna come."

He pulled his hand away. "Nope."

"*Fuck.*"

"It must suck to be you right now."

It did. It did suck to be her. The only consolation was knowing that eventually she *would* come, and it would be great, but that did nothing to satisfy the screaming id-monster in her brain that wanted to come *now now now*.

"That was a close one," Logan said, way too cheerily. God, was there anything worse than a cheerful sadist? "I was gonna put you on the bed, but I don't think we're there yet and that won't help either of us hold out. So I hope you're good to stand up a while longer."

"I'm good, sir." She hoped her voice didn't betray her uncertainty. It felt like they'd been there forever, but it was probably more like ten minutes. She been in sessions at the club that lasted hours. It was the up-and-down that was fucking with her stamina. The pauses and tenderness and kissing. And the knowledge, always threatening to pull her back from subspace, that the better things went with Logan, the more she was setting herself up for an emotional fall. She trusted Logan not to hurt her, trusted him completely. But she no longer trusted herself.

He chose the riding crop next. A *pop* here, a *pop* there. A rain of feathery, stinging taps against the flogger-reddened flesh of her thighs. Then he unclipped the cuffs, turned her back to the bed, resecured her with her hands behind her back . . . and started on her front side. A clean canvas, mostly.

After the first few whipping smacks to her legs, he made a time-out sign and rummaged through his bag again, finally coming up with a plain black mask. He chatted as he tucked her hair behind her ears and slipped the mask into place over her eyes, adjusting it carefully so it sat comfortably. "I have a really nice one in storage. Fitted, blocks out *all* the light. But this will work well enough so you can't see where the next one's coming from."

More catnip. With her eyes covered, she let herself relax further into the scene. Into helplessness. Letting in the pain, becoming a sponge to absorb whatever Logan needed to pour into her. At first she waited, listening. He was doing something else by the dresser, and she heard some metallic *click*s. Then he returned, running a hand down her leg to her ankle and fastening a cuff there. Another metallic *clank* and scrape; something was attached to it. She figured out it was the spreader bar as he was securing the other ankle and nudging her stance wider.

"More," he snapped, when she didn't move her foot far enough. "I need a good two feet of clearance here." Then she felt him clipping the cuffs to the bar. She used the bedpost for support, tested the new restraint. It was solid, holding her legs wide, making her more vulnerable.

Good. So good.

More crop strikes fell, lighting up her inner thighs. A sequence of quick, shockingly painful taps to her clit and pussy. Light, playful smacks on her belly—not enough to hurt, only enough to let her know where he was headed. He would back off every so often, though, then sneak back in with something unexpected. A hard strike to the leg or hip. A tickle at the arch of her foot, nearly making her fall over as she squirmed to get away from the sensation.

"Oooh, yellow, yellow!"

"Seriously?"

"No tickling, I don't like tickling." Her whole body crawled, as if her skin was trying to escape the abhorrent sensation. "It's not hot. Please tell me you aren't into it."

Logan laughed, somewhere in the vicinity of her knee. She could feel the puff of air, then the brush of his lips against her quad muscle. He reached down to her foot and pressed firmly where he'd tickled, rubbing the spot for a few seconds until she relaxed.

"I'm not into it," he reassured her as he let go. "Good to know if there's ever a time for punishment, maybe."

Whomp, straight to the emotions. "This is a one-off, remember?"

He sucked air in sharply. "Uh, yeah. Right. Okay, where were we? Oh well, since I'm down here, I've been meaning to do this . . ."

He licked her inner thigh, flicking his tongue upward to the spot where he'd pinched her earlier. In his office, a lifetime ago. Pinching wasn't enough, apparently. He suckled at the sore flesh, worrying it with his tongue. Then he rested his teeth there, making his intention clear, letting her anticipation build, before he started to bite down.

The pain deepened until a buzz shot up her spine, exploding brilliantly in her skull. The world's edges faded; behind the mask, she saw stars. When he finally eased up, he moved his mouth only inches, humming a pleased note as he settled his lips over her clit and flattened his tongue against it. Worked it until she started to moan. Then he pressed a few soft kisses there and vanished again, leaving her in the dark with her pain and need.

She cried out—she was hoarse, she must have been making noise during the session and not been aware of it—and he stroked her flank. Soothing, gentling . . . then flicking one of her nipples with the tip of the crop. Then the other. Back and forth at random, sometimes the nipple, sometimes the sensitive flesh above or below. Avoiding the existing bite mark, so she knew he was building up to that.

When he finally whacked her there, it was hard and sharp and perfect and she swayed against her cuffs, almost falling over. He waited for her to recover, then smacked the same spot again. She jerked, and started to shake, but stayed on her feet.

He pulled the third blow, it was barely a hit at all. Or possibly that was just her spaced-out brain, turning the pain into something else. Funneling it into the great vortex of need that swamped her when Logan stepped close to her again and cupped her face between his hands.

"Nice," he whispered, then kissed her slowly. Sweetly. If they'd dated in high school, he couldn't have kissed her any more sweetly than this after a perfect first date.

That could have happened. He could have come back from college, they could have seen each other in Minnie's and shared a look and a slice of pie and just *known*. They could have dated long-distance during college, then gotten married and had a house somewhere and babies. She could have gone to Houston. They could have been starting this crazy dude ranch enterprise together. All that could so easily be her life right now. Their life.

Would he still be kissing her like this, if that had happened? Would she still be cuffed to the bed? Or would the kink have fallen by the wayside with the onslaught of kids and mortgages and adulting? Would they have this same spark? Mindy told herself she was glad they hadn't been high school sweethearts, because there was no way they would have this heat, this crazy energy together, if they'd worn it out on housework and talking about whose health insurance was better. But a flicker from deeper inside her told her another truth: If she had been his all along, Logan would still kiss her like this every damn day.

But that wasn't their history. Now she would always be the one who'd tried to hoodwink him into a land deal. She would always have guilt about that... wouldn't she? And he could only take so much of that back out of her hide.

She kissed him back, sighing softly into his gentle mouth, and when he pressed his teeth into her bottom lip again she started to cry. The mask hid the tears, but she couldn't keep the sniffling a secret. Logan pulled the mask away, tossing it to one side, and brushed his thumbs over her cheeks, obvious concern in his face.

"I always do this," she lied. "It's fine."

He looked skeptical, but after a second he shrugged and kissed her again. "Okay. Time for bed."

He unhooked her feet from the spreader bar first, tossing it onto the covers, then frowning and leaving her side for a moment while he whipped the quilt and blanket from the bed to the floor so only the sheets and pillows remained. Then the wrists. He left all the cuffs in place.

When he pointed to the center of the bed, Mindy crawled up, feeling the pain in every inch of her body. It ached like a fever, making her skin feel taut and oversensitive and too full of every type of feeling. The bed squeaked with each movement. She trembled on all fours until Logan yanked two pillows, settled them under her hips, and pushed her shoulders down. Mindy stretched out gratefully, the top half of her body sinking into the mattress while her butt stayed high, her legs spread.

After yanking his lounge pants off, Logan pulled the lead ropes from the dresser and secured them around the headboard, then clipped Mindy's wrist cuffs to the ends. The ropes were soft, thick nylon, and felt good under her hands when she gripped them. Sturdy. Inescapable. Safe.

The whole room was safe—the ancient-seeming iron bed, the plush mattress, the man who knelt behind her, chucking a strip of wrapped condoms and a lube bottle down as he sat. Even the Lucite rod he was holding didn't scare her. He might cause any number of injuries to her *body*, but he would never *harm* her. Mindy had never trusted a Dom so quickly, so easily. But then, none of her former Doms had ever taught her the quadratic equation. None of their moms had ever sold her homecoming mums or bought her fund-raiser candy. She'd never helped any of them scold their little brothers for inappropriate remarks.

Logan rubbed the makeshift cane over the ball of one of her feet—too firmly to tickle—then tapped it there. "Is this okay?"

"Yes, sir." She could hear the tears in her voice, and hoped he would ignore them. The melancholy would leave her when the pain came back.

He smacked the ball of her foot harder, a quick, stinging blow. Again and again, varying the spot but never the pressure. Ball, heel, the sole to the side of the arch. He covered the bottom of that foot, then left it for the other side. By the time he was done, both her feet were throbbing and sensitive but she was so relaxed otherwise she could have almost gone to sleep if she hadn't know what was coming.

He wouldn't have brought the cane to bed only for a round of light bastinado. When he left off her feet, Mindy braced for impact higher up. She didn't get it, but wasn't disappointed. Instead, Logan put the implement of destruction to one side and raked his nails over her ass and thighs again, lighting up all the spots where the pain had started to ease.

"It's nice and red, but you need some more accent marks back here before I fuck you."

She tried to laugh, but the sound she produced was more like a strangled *Gaaah*. Logan had shifted his attention to her pussy, stroking his fingers alongside it, spreading her wide, slipping one thumb inside her while his fingers fanned over her clit. She felt swollen, exposed, ready to ignite at any second. He rocked his hand back and forth until she moaned and ground against his touch. It was irresistible. And maybe this was it, maybe this was when she'd finally get to come.

She lost herself in it, pumping her hips harder, fucking herself on his hand, until the swirling pleasure inside her focused behind her clit like a shimmering ball of potential.

When he yanked his hand away and smacked her ass, she started crying again. "Pleeeeease, sir? Please?" She yanked on the cuffs. So close. She was dizzy with how close she'd been.

He chuckled and retrieved the cane, moving a little to one side of her. "You can come when I do. Or thereabouts."

"Please?" But it was just a hopeless whisper into her pillow. Followed hard by a wordless scream as the cane met her sore ass. An expert blow or a very lucky one, right across both cheeks. The next one angled across the back of one thigh, and she bucked and sobbed. The movement brought her clit against the pillow, and she tried to get enough leverage against the soft surface to bring herself off, riding the pain and pleasure as they combined inside her.

"Not yet, Melinda." Logan hauled her hips up, repositioning her. "You know better. I hope you know better, anyway. What do you say?"

"S—sorry, sir."

"I don't believe you." He braced one hand on her hip and lined the cane up against the other cheek, tapping once to show his intent. "Let me hear how sorry you are."

He brought it down hard on the meat of her ass, and she screamed her apology as the agony rattled her skull. Bliss, it was bliss, being filled entirely by that pain. It was *life*.

Slick, careful fingers brushed her pussy. Then cool liquid, trickling down. And then Logan's hands were on her hips, and his cock was pressing for entrance, and she pushed back to meet him, and it was everything. He completed her.

She'd been too keyed up, too ready for too long. She started to come before he was even fully inside, a slow implosion of delight she was powerless to stop. She tried, clawing at the sheet, making a futile effort not to move.

"Sorry, sorry, oh fuck, sorry, gonna nnngggghhh—"

"Go. Do it. Fuck, yes." He slapped her haunch and started thrusting hard. Fast, deep, wild, and absolutely perfect.

Mindy shattered. Her whole body spasmed as the orgasm took over, rolled through her, shook her soul like a rag doll. Then left her grudgingly, first with a series of aftershocks, then with a flash of sensitivity so keen that every movement of Logan's cock inside her became a swift agony of remembered pleasure.

He came with a shout, a curse, then leaned over her, shuddering and still working his hips. Then moving more fitfully, slowing his manic pace to a crawl, and finally to a stop.

They breathed at each other like the winded animals they were, for a period of time Mindy felt in no state to measure. Could have been seconds. Could have been forever. Eventually Logan leaned over and dropped a kiss to her shoulder.

"Holy fucking fuck." He pulled back, groaning, and worked his way off the squeaky bed. Dealing with the condom, Mindy assumed.

She might have fallen asleep. The next thing she registered was him unclipping her wrist cuffs from the leads, and starting to unbuckle one.

"Want 'em on," she mumbled. They felt so good.

He rubbed the back of her hand, then lifted it to his lips for a quick kiss. "We need to take the wrist ones off, they might leave some marks if you have them on all night. But you can keep the ankle cuffs, okay?"

She sighed. "'Kay. Thank you, sir." For everything. For the beating, and the astonishingly good sex. For remembering she needed to keep her arms unmarked. For taking her out of herself, however shortly. She didn't have the words to say it out loud. She barely remembered her own name.

Then she was startled awake again by a warm, wet cloth being stroked between her legs. Thunder rumbled and the windows lit up, rain pelting the glass as though the storm was gaining a second wind.

Then she was snuggling a pillow, while a quilt was tucked securely around her, with an extra few careful tucks around her throbbing feet.

Then Logan was under the blanket with her, spooned against her back with his arm over her waist and his lips pressed to her hair.

Chapter Twelve

It was probably not the best way to run a business.

Logan was exhausted the next morning, and not just because of the hours of deviant carousing. It was all the nights before that with almost no sleep, as he'd stared at spreadsheets, at all the unpromising numbers. He'd studied the figures in every spare moment, he'd tried to adjust as he went along now that people were actually *here* and he could see how it all worked. He'd done everything but cartwheels trying to entertain the customers, and he could only hope it would be enough to somehow conjure up more business. And he really should have either done more of the same, or gotten some damn sleep for once, instead of kinky shenanigans.

At least he was too distracted to be nervous about satisfying the rest of the guests anymore. He only really cared about pleasing one of them, and he was pretty convinced that Tuesday had its own time-space continuum because it seemed to last *forever*. After dark, after everybody else was asleep, that was when he could get more alone time with Mindy. Until then, it was all excruciating wait time and trying to restrain himself from grabbing her ass.

He succeeded. Mostly.

The morning had been . . . weird. She'd been gone from the bed when he woke up to his alarm, and his heart had plummeted like a stone. No note, no good-bye text. She'd said she planned to go, and she was gone, and everything was terrible.

But when he walked down to help Robert and Diego set up breakfast, there she was. Laughing, carrying a stack of plates. Wearing a blue "Bolero" T-shirt, probably the one she'd mentioned the night before when he'd offered her the robe instead.

The guys barely spared him a glance. He had no idea what backstory Mindy had given for being in the main house so early, or what his two friends-turned-employees knew about their relationship other than what Robert had already witnessed. So he could only silently thank her for staying, and start setting out the silverware.

She vanished after eating a stuffed three-egg omelette and half a pig's worth of bacon, and Logan figured that was it. She'd pack and go and that would be the end of the strange saga of Logan and Mindy and their kinky one-night stand. He took a group out for a trail ride, and tried to concentrate on the paying customers he *wouldn't* give an eyetooth to scene with one more time. The folks he *didn't* want to fall asleep spooning against.

When she showed up at his and Lamar's bullwhip demonstration after lunch, he was almost annoyed. He wanted closure—if she was set to leave, she should just leave. It hit him like a brick, halfway through whipping a line of cans off the top of the corral fence: Maybe she wasn't leaving.

He didn't miss a beat. Half a dozen cans, half a dozen strokes, just like he'd practiced it a million times. The guests applauded and whistled, Logan took a bow. But when Lamar stepped in to do his bit—a lasso trick, for a sneak preview of the next day's entertainment—Logan held up his hand.

"Who wants an encore?"

The obliging group responded favorably, and Logan held up a hand to shade his eyes, pretending to scan the crowd. "Can I get a volunteer . . . oh, you there, the young lady in blue. Step right this way, please."

Mindy lifted her eyebrows at him but obliged, walking to the front to stand next to him.

"Waiver?" Lamar muttered, shaking his head.

Logan shrugged. "This ain't my first rodeo."

Or Mindy's. While he spoke to his stable hand, she took an elastic off her wrist and put her hair in a low ponytail, securing it from the fitful wind. Logan flipped it forward of her shoulder and positioned her with her back to the audience, her hands clasped in front of her. He lifted her chin with a finger, and made the mistake of eye contact. Time swirled, the audience faded, he almost leaned in for a kiss then caught himself and took his hand away. Found the nearest can, brushed the dust off it, and placed it carefully on top of Mindy's head.

He caught her eye again. "Don't move until I say."

A smile played around the corners of her mouth. "Yes, sir."

God.

He paced off the range, pretending to count his steps for the crowd as if he actually had to think about it. It was simple math, really, just measurement and knowing the length of his own stride, practicing until he could do it consistently. But the whip was loud, and potentially dangerous, and people *loved* the drama of it. This was really no different from doing a demo at a club or play party. Except it was outdoors, which was nice because it gave him a lot of room. And nobody was in fetish gear. There were zero Doms secretly fondling their subs in this crowd. Exactly no naked breasts or buttocks were on display. It was also—as far as he could tell—a dildo-free environment. But other than that, pretty much exactly the same as a club.

Better than a club, really, for all those reasons. What a shame they couldn't just turn the whole place into an open-air kink free-for-all. Forget selling logo caps and make a fortune price-gouging participants on sunscreen and bug spray.

He turned and assessed Mindy's back. Her ruddy hair contrasted sharply with the blue shirt, but his eyes were drawn down. Her ass was such a tempting target he had to wrench his gaze up to the can on top of her head.

"*Can* I do it?" he called, smirking at the inevitable groans and swishing the whip suggestively a few times to loosen his arm. "I think I can, I think I can, I think I—" *Whip!*

The can flew off, and the crowd went wild. Logan allowed himself a mental pat on the back. Mindy stood completely still. He couldn't help himself.

"A round of applause for my victim—I mean, assistant! Mindy, everyone!"

They clapped, but she didn't move a muscle. She was smart. And well trained, sweet Jesus, so well trained. Logan grinned and swished his whip around again.

"Clever girl," he called out. *Swish, swish.*

She yelled out, "Ha!"

Whip! Crack!

"*Eep!*"

It had snapped a good foot from her ass, but close enough she *had* to have had a moment of panic. That was built into people. Only training could explain her ability to keep from flinching. But whoever had bullwhipped her hadn't trained the adorable fear-squeak out of her. What would she sound like when the whip actually connected?

He had to stop, or he was going to be sporting wood in front of a crowd of paying customers. Not his jam. "*Now* you can move! Thank you for volunteering!"

Mindy turned with a grin and took a bow, then waited a beat and stuck her tongue out at Logan. The audience ate it up.

Logan remembered the noise she'd made when he'd bitten her tongue. And the way she used to grin and whoop when she finally got a math concept right and demonstrated it perfectly. And how she hadn't let him kill the spider. All of the memories, old and new, jumbled together as if she'd been there by his side the whole time.

When the crowd trailed after Lamar to hear Ethan talk about nineteenth-century blacksmithing techniques, Logan held Mindy back with a hand on her arm.

"I thought you were leaving."

She eyed the backs of the other guests as if she would rather join them than have this talk, then turned to him with a cockeyed smile and an exaggerated shrug. "I thought so, too. I don't know what I'm doing." Her face went serious, and she repeated it earnestly, with a whole new weight. "I don't know what I'm doing."

"Me, I hope." Probably the wrong tone, but what the hell.

"Sure. But *why*?" Then she must've realized how that sounded, and frantically waved her hands, shaking her head. "No, no, I didn't mean it like that, you were great. I mean, like . . . at what cost. Oh God, no, that's—"

"It's cool." He stilled her hands with his, then released them before he got tempted to pull her in for a hug. "I knew what you meant. Sort of. It's weird."

"It *is* weird."

"Unexpected."

"For sure. *So* not how I planned all this."

A tiny voice in the back of his head questioned that, and he hated himself for it. She'd expected—what was it again?—a "pathetic, balding, drugstore cowboy." That was who she'd planned to flirt with if she needed to. He didn't like to toot his own horn, but he figured he was at least some level of upgrade. And her preferred flavor of dominant to boot, apparently.

That was where his suspicion crumbled. He could believe flirting, maybe even sex, to get a deal. Not from Mindy, necessarily, but in general—he knew it happened, that men and women alike resorted to that as a business tactic in all sorts of fields where people would never expect it. The news was full of those stories. But once the whips came out . . . there was no way she would've gone that far on the off chance he was still down for a deal. The kink was real, at the very least.

If she was staying, he probably ought to assume it was for more of that.

But that wasn't why he *wanted* her to stay. She fit in at Hilltop. She lit the place up. A woman's touch, maybe? Hell if he knew, but something had been missing in the mix of the whole setup until she'd started helping out. He would have considered asking her to stay even if it weren't about wanting to take her on a date or something— someplace away from here, to see whether their connection lasted outside the perimeters of the ranch. And even if it weren't for the kink, which had been . . .

Well, it hadn't all gone completely smoothly, in truth. Something they had to address if there were to be more scenes.

He reached for her arm again, sliding his fingers down to encircle her wrist. Not to make her feel trapped, but to help her feel safe. "Mindy, why were you really crying last night?"

It was the pause that did it. That was a giveaway. If she'd just said, "I always do that," without thinking it over first, he'd have bought it. As it was . . . no.

"It's better to have things out in the open," he reminded her.

"If you must know, your magic spooge got to me a little."

"Why am I not flattered?"

"Crushing self-esteem issues stemming from an unhappy childhood?"

He took her other wrist, shackling her firmly. "Melinda. Can you just be honest with me? If you don't want to tell me, say you don't want to tell me. Say it's none of my business. But if it was because of something I did, I need to know."

She'd already been looking down, avoiding his gaze. Now she glanced off to the side. He wanted to tell her never, ever to play poker. She was one big tell. He couldn't bring himself to believe anybody had an act this good.

"I lied . . . a little."

"About . . . ?" He tried to ignore the sinking feeling in his chest.

"I wasn't homesick for Dallas," she explained. "I'm homesick for *here*. For Bolero. These trees, dirt this color, the way it all smells, the damn pie at Minnie's. Just . . . all of it."

He tried to piece it together, but just couldn't. "Okay. But. You're *here*."

"I know. That's the problem." She finally looked up, her brown eyes almost amber in the late afternoon sunlight. "I'm here, but I'm not supposed to be. And I have to go back home. That's hanging over me. Once I realized how much I wanted to stay here, and that I *couldn't* stay, I thought I'd get it over with fast, like ripping off a Band-Aid. Then the storm happened. And I thought, well, I should have seen that coming. So did I set myself up by not keeping a close enough eye on the weather? Then I ran up to say good-bye because I thought it would be really shitty to leave without saying goodbye. And of course you weren't going to let me run back out of there with the sky falling. I knew that *afterward*. It was so obvious *afterward*, but at the time I felt like I was doing the right thing. Then that scene, and the whole thing, it was . . . good, *really good*, and it's not that I *want* to leave. It's that I feel like I'd be smarter to? But I don't *want* to."

Her eyes pleaded with him, and he wished like anything he had an easy answer for her. Something to make it all okay. But he didn't want her to leave, either, so he wasn't really qualified to advise her. He wanted her to stay. Or at least to come back. That much, he'd figured out, and he didn't care how stupid or ill-advised it was. "That's a lot to sort through."

"I know. So when I say I don't know what I'm doing, I mean all of that. It's such a mess. *I'm* a mess."

Her wrists felt vulnerable in his hands—strong, but only relatively so. He could snap her if he wanted to. But all he really wanted was to help her feel better about whatever she decided. He was too sleep-deprived to feel confident he could give good counsel, but he had to try. "It's kind of late now. If you start this late, you'll be driving at least some of the way in the dark. So I really hope you at least stay tonight and hit the road tomorrow. And we can maybe talk more after supper, and get to feeling better about at least some things?"

After a second or so, she nodded. "That makes sense."

He told himself not to do it. *Don't do it, man. Do NOT.* But he did it. "You know the isolation stalls? The old barn, I mean? Ethan went through there earlier, swept out the creepy-crawlies, but he ended up putting his horses in the big barn." The ranch was full of old and new versions of the same thing—sturdy old rock buildings in need of repair, and newer structures his grandparents had installed a few decades ago, when their customers had found the old ones too outdated. Now the native rock was part of the retro appeal, so Logan was looking into restoring everything. "He said the ceiling beams are actually in pretty good shape. In terms of load-bearing."

Mindy planted one toe and swiveled her heel back and forth, grinding a circle in the dust. "I assume you're not just telling me this because you're interested in architecture? Oh . . . he ties people up. So you mean some suspension, in the barn? Sure, I could go for that. Not both of you, though. That would be weird."

"No, no, gross. He's my brother. We don't . . . well, not if there's any sex involved. We've done, like, suspension demos where I've helped him rig some things that need two people."

"The barn would actually be a wonderful place for suspension demos. So atmospheric, you know? You could charge admission. There's plenty of room for spectators. Of course, you wouldn't want to do it while you had the regular guests here."

Logan chuckled. "That'd be one way to make some more money. I'll have to keep that in mind. But . . . no. I just thought we could finish what we started the day you got here." He ran his thumbs over her wrists, tracing the delicate veins and tendons. Imagining them bound in elegant twists of rope.

"In the tack room, you mean?" She looked up shyly—but at least not upset anymore. "You have a thing for barns, sir."

"Yeehaw," he confirmed.

She looked down again for a few seconds, then nodded slowly. "Yeah. Okay. Just name the time."

The atmosphere was perfect. Mindy stared up into the rafters, trying to pick out details above the point from which she hung by one foot. Everything was too dark, however, outside the pool of light from the lantern Logan had brought. The old barn wasn't wired for electricity—that was one of many needed improvements. For years, it had been used only when they needed to isolate a fractious stallion or an ill horse.

"And the occasional pig or cow," Logan added, sighing over a hank of rope he'd been casting out then rewrapping for the past few minutes. "God, this thing just won't lie smooth. Yeah, Memaw and Papaw used to keep a little herd out here, and some other animals, for authenticity. You doin' okay?"

"Super." She hauled on the section of rope that looped up through the suspension ring, pulling herself vertical again. "I wish I could remember the three-point self-suspension thing. It's chest and both feet, but there's a certain order to how you get yourself into it. I can stay in that one forever."

Logan looked up. "Ethan would know."

She worked her foot against the pressure of the rope, shifting her weight to get more comfortable. "You really like him around for this stuff, don't you? Should I be concerned?" The loops around her torso were compressing, but not dangerously so. At least she'd remembered that part of the process correctly.

"You're fully clothed and suspending yourself. There is nothing sexual about this situation."

"You sound a little grumpy about that, sir." She grinned and inverted again, flipping her hair down against the old mattress Logan had dragged from the main house to provide some cushion under the suspension point. "Self-suspension is so much fun." It really was. It always cheered her up, made her feel like a trapeze artist in the circus. Glamorous, with mad skills. Even if she was only doing the simplest tricks.

"So is tying other people up when they're naked."

"True. Fair enough. You didn't press very hard for that, though." She was vaguely concerned that he hadn't. But she wasn't sure if the pall currently shadowing his expression was frustration with her, general fatigue, moodiness, or something else. She didn't know him well enough to know the difference.

She unknotted the loose end from her rope-wrapped midsection and lowered herself carefully onto the mattress, head then shoulders then back. From that position she could look up at Logan as he sat cross-legged at one end of the mattress.

He tied off the wrap he'd been working on and tossed it down in front of his legs. "Eh, fuck it. It isn't perfect, so what?"

Mindy rolled to a sitting position and eased the loops of rope down from her rib cage. She left her foot bound, so she wouldn't have to retie it in case the three-point process came back to her. "You look tired. I won't have any hard feelings if you want to call it a night."

He opened his mouth as if to protest, then shook his head and chuckled. "I'm pretty wiped out. This is my new normal, though, I guess. Not last night, as such, but the whole thing. Staying up too late to work out details, try to get new ideas. I don't know . . ." He picked the bundle of rope up and stroked the loops thoughtfully.

"I'm exhausted, too," she admitted, rolling on her side to face him and propping herself on one elbow. "I feel like I've put in a year's worth of good honest work, these past few days. Plus all this fresh country air, my lungs don't know what to do with themselves. So thank you for all that."

He shot her a sardonic smile. "You aren't exactly on the standard vacation package."

"True, true. You could probably make a fortune selling my vacation package to the right clientele, though." She sifted her fingers through the loops on the opposite end of his rope bundle. It was hemp, soft and beautifully dyed, almost the same cobalt blue as her shirt. "This is lovely stuff, by the way."

"Thanks. Ethan made it."

"Seriously? Wow."

"He and a friend make it and sell a little online, and at some of the local conventions when they can get there. The friend also makes wooden toys, that's the primary business. The rope's just a sideline. They don't have space to do anything over fifty feet, or dye in anything other than solid colors, which limits them."

She gestured around them. "Why doesn't he just do it here? All the space in the world. You could have an off-limits area so the vanilla dude ranchers don't ever suspect there's a kinky bondage rope factory or . . . however you make it."

Logan pursed his lips. "That's actually not a bad idea. He's talked about moving out here anyway, he wants to build one of those little house trailer things that look like cottages."

"A tiny house?" She loved them. Wouldn't want to live in one, but she thought the idea was great for the right person.

"Yeah. He says I should open up for people to park them here. Rent the land. Another way to make money. I just . . ." He shrugged and rested his elbows on his knees, his chin in his hands.

"You don't want to spoil it. I get it now. I really do." It broke her heart. Riding and walking all over the ranch the past few days, she had seen the raw beauty of the place. She didn't want it spoiled, either. Just thinking about what would have happened if she'd succeeded in getting him to sign the lease made her physically ill.

Or possibly that was spending too long in an inverted suspension. But still.

"You're the last person I should be telling this to." He leaned his forehead into his hands. "But I don't know if I can make this work."

He wasn't talking about their relationship. Or lack thereof. For a second she was tempted to pretend she thought that was what he'd meant, but then she couldn't take the thought of any more subterfuge.

She stroked his hair, combing her fingers through the waves. "Maybe look at the numbers when you're not so worn out?"

He shrugged. "I've looked. Ethan's looked. Our accountant is still looking but hasn't sounded that hopeful. There are just too many big, established ranches out here that we can't compete with on cost, and we haven't come up with a unique draw. Our preliminary numbers looked better, but there were a lot of factors we didn't know to account for. Seasonal cost changes, some of the operating expenses we learned about as we did the initial restoration. We had some overruns there, too. To do it the way we really wanted, go high-end and cater to a boutique crowd like I wanted, work the hunting angle Chet suggested, work the living-history angle with some cattle and a full vintage blacksmith shop like Ethan wants, we'd need a lot of money and a lot of time. And we won't make enough in the meantime to get us there. It'll be a few years of barely breaking even and then the place sliding downhill because we don't have the capital to improve it to the point where it could make us more money. And . . . ugh. The whole thing is turning into a train wreck."

It was the longest speech she'd ever heard him make, and she wished she could make it better, but she couldn't. She could only offer some pleasant distraction. "So. You want to walk me back to my place, maybe fool around a little?"

Logan tapped his fingers against his forehead. "Maaayyyybeee."

Taking it as a yes, she stood and stretched, wincing as her various bruises and welts made themselves known. She reached a hand down and after a second he took it, allowing her to pull him to his feet. He continued the motion straight into a hug, picking her up gently by the waist and swinging her around once before kissing her on the cheek.

"What was that for?"

"Letting me vent." He set her down, only to bend, grab her by the knees and shoulders, and quickly scoop her into his arms. This time, he kissed her hard on the mouth, not letting up until they were both breathless. "That was for offering to make me feel better with sex."

"Any time." She said it automatically, senses still reeling from the sensation of his lips and tongue and end-of-the-day stubble. She didn't expect him to take her up on it.

"Maybe next time we could bolt the door in here and get you naked. Probably need a gag so you won't frighten the guests when I bullwhip you, though."

"Next time? Logan . . ." She kicked her feet, and he set her down again.

But he didn't let up on the topic. "Yeah. Next time. Like when you drive down here some time from Dallas. To visit. I could take you to Minnie's for pie and everything. We could go to a drive-in movie." He seemed so certain about the next time, she found herself believing him. At least enough to pretend for tonight.

She sat and started unwrapping the rope from her foot and ankle. The marks were perfect, pink and deep and clear. She wondered what the ones on her torso looked like. "The drive-in hasn't been there since we were in high school."

"It's still there," he corrected her, throwing the rest of the rope into his bag. "They just don't show movies anymore. And most of the screen is gone. But I figured we could park and watch something on a tablet. Bring some popcorn. Make a night of it."

"Crazy." She flung the foot rope at him, and he caught it deftly.

"But cute. Admit it."

"Yeah. You have a certain appeal." All-American cowboy engineer sadist appeal. Which was apparently her Kryptonite.

He took her hand firmly on the walk back to the cabin. He pointed out some stars—not just the Pleiades and Orion's Belt and the Big Dipper, like most guys who thought girls couldn't possibly already know these things, but some ones she actually didn't know. When they arrived at the cabin, he greeted Moose with solemn dignity and a promise to maintain detente.

Mindy excused herself to go to the restroom and when she came back out, stark naked, ready to show Logan her lovely new rope marks, he was facedown on her bed. Not quite snoring. But not exactly *not* snoring.

At least his boots were off.

She set a five o'clock alarm on her phone, turned off the lights, flipped a blanket over them both, and cuddled against his side like she belonged there.

Chapter Thirteen

They all agreed they'd hit it lucky with the weather—the drop in temperature after the storm had held, so it was cool and breezy the next day, and promised to be down in the high fifties after nightfall.

About half of the guests were already gathered around the fire pit, working on setting up the first bonfire. Floyd Gordon had no idea how to stack wood for a fire, but that was okay. Everybody was still having a good time.

Mindy handed Floyd another split log from the pile behind the bench, and tried not to giggle at the faces Logan's cousin Chet was making behind the guy's back. Not to mock, but if Chet's jaw got any tighter or his eyes any squintier, he'd turn into a cartoon character. The poor guy was so frustrated watching the inept fire-building that Mindy expected steam to burst out of his ears any second.

Finally, she couldn't take it anymore. "Hey, Chet. Uh, Sheriff Garcia. I heard Robert mention earlier he had some old newspapers saved up. Have you seen him anywhere recently?"

Chet turned his scowl on her, and for a second she thought she was about to reap the whirlwind. Then he nodded sternly, seeming to get the hint that she was trying to give him an out. "Chet will do. In this setting. I will seek Robert out. Excuse me."

He strode off like a mountain man on a mission to hunt down the last grizzly and wrestle it to death. That was a happier look for him than watching Floyd lay an inadequate fire.

"Thank you, sweetheart. I thought he was gonna stare a damn hole in my back."

She turned back to Floyd, giggling, wondering why it really didn't bother her to have Floyd call her sweetheart when back in Dallas she'd have had to leave the room to cool down for half an hour if she'd heard that. "Let's hope he takes a while to twist up a lot of kindling out of that paper. It'll give you time to clear the area so you can't see him sneak back and move your logs around."

Floyd's wife, Thelma, cackled. "I have to do that with the Christmas tree tinsel every year. He's used to it."

"I can *hear* you, you know!" Floyd placed the last log in the careful stack, then stepped back, brushing his hands off on his thighs. "Ah, hell with it anyway. It's fire, not rocket science. My experience, if the wood's dry, it'll catch and do just fine. If ol' Chet wants to switch it up, that'll do just fine, too." He joined his wife and one of the other guests, Marlene Jackson, on their bench.

Mindy had seen good ol' boys come to blows over less serious matters than how to stack a campfire, but she kept her skepticism to herself. At least there was no beer in the equation. Yet.

The Delgados, Bob Jackson, and Mary Havlicek were all still out on their last trail ride of the week. It was an hour or so until sunset, which meant Lamar would be leading the riders back from the High Trail any minute. The smell of searing meat drifted over from the big barbecue grill next to the kitchen door. Beneath that, a hint of white jasmine floated on the air; the vines ran rampant in the as-yet-untamed back garden. Cicadas churred. Some sort of insect or frog made a gentle but insistent peeping noise. The Gordons and their new friend talked companionably, laughing softly, seeming just as loath to disturb the quiet as Mindy was.

Mindy looked at the fire pit, marveling that she'd helped build it just a few days earlier. She felt like she'd been at Hilltop Ranch forever. She couldn't imagine being back at work Monday, or even driving through Dallas to get to her apartment. Instead of trying—which made her shoulders tense and her belly ache—she let the late afternoon peace settle over her. The moment was fleeting and bittersweet, but she'd take what she could get.

"Mindy, where'd Logan get off to?" Marlene asked.

"Front porch." She didn't need to look over to the house to answer. "He had some invoices he needed to go over before supper. Is there something I can help you with? I'd be happy to go ask—"

"Oh no, no. Just wondering. You let him work for now so he can be free to eat later."

Thelma poked Marlene in the side. "She'd be happy to go ask him, if you need something."

"I'll bet. But I don't need anything." Marlene shouldered her friend back, then shook her head and smiled at Mindy. "Don't you mind us. But the two of you are very cute together. Have you set the date yet?"

Mindy's face flushed so fast and hot she thought her skin might literally be smoking. "Uh . . ."

"Mar*lene*," Thelma chided. "She doesn't have a *ring*."

Oh, help me, Jesus. "We're really just friends. I live in Dallas. It's not . . . not that kind of deal." She was tempted to tell them exactly what kind of deal it was. She had to get out before she blurted something about floggers and domination. "I'll just go check on dinner."

As she backed away then turned and ran, she could hear Thelma and Marlene chiding each other. She didn't care. The only thing that mattered was to get away from the gossip danger zone. Even if that meant marching straight to the porch of the main house, where Logan sat on the creaky swing with a stack of papers and his laptop.

On the way she passed Chet and Diego, staggering back toward the fire pit with a galvanized tub full of ice and longnecks. They were studiously avoiding eye contact, and Chet's jaw was clenched again. Mindy had no idea what the story was there, but she could tell there was one, and likely a doozy. She'd remembered them as good friends from way back. Diego was a masochist, she'd gleaned that much on this visit. Chet seemed like such an obvious Dom. But who knew, maybe they'd just fallen out over high school football or politics or something.

Logan spotted her on the steps and closed his laptop, stacking it on top of the papers on the bench, as she reached the porch. "Fire all ready to go?"

"Waiting for the inaugural match. And I guess for the trail ride to be over, so everybody can see. Did Lamar already radio Robert? I smelled the barbecue firing up."

"Yep. Any chance you'd help Lamar put the horses up? That way maybe folks can get their dinner a little faster and we can get the whole fire party on before it's full dark."

"I don't count as 'folks'?" she teased. "Sure, no problem."

"I could *order* you to do it." He fake-frowned, as if he were seriously considering it, and started the swing in motion with both feet.

"Well, you know, then if I screwed up you'd have to put me over your knee in front of all those people, and the jig would be up, so it's probably for the best if you don't. I'll volunteer. Just save me some ribs, please."

"Yes, ma'am. Can I put you over my knee later, though?"

Mindy smiled and glanced out over the porch rail. Nobody was nearby. Probably everybody wanted to give the "lovebirds" their space. "I don't think I have any unblemished real estate left back there, but I guess you could try."

"Maybe next time."

"Logan . . ." She hadn't put her foot down last night, which was probably a mistake. Facing him again, she set her shoulders and forced herself to shut that prospect down. "I'm going back to Dallas tomorrow, and I'm going to stay in Dallas. I can't come back here. It wouldn't be healthy for me."

He crossed his arms across his chest, squinting at her, and she suddenly saw the family resemblance between him and Chet.

"You said yourself you felt homesick for this place. That means it's part of you. And this week . . . you look so at home here. Like you belong here. And you seem *happy* here, and miserable about going back to Dallas. For which I don't blame you. But I don't see how coming to a place where you feel more like yourself isn't healthy."

She wanted him to be wrong. Clearly and demonstrably wrong. It infuriated her that he wasn't. "I was happy on vacation. But I have to look at the long term. I thought, I don't know, that I'd reinvented myself after I left here. That I was somebody new and better now. Like a swan. But from the first day back here I've done nothing but come smack up against the fact that I'm still just the ugly duckling. I was never the swan. So what have I been doing all this for? I feel like coming back will only remind me of that. Make me feel bad about what I've accomplished."

Logan chuckled, a little puff of air that spoke of wistfulness as much as it did amusement. "Have you ever met a swan? I don't recommend it. They're pretty from a distance but up close they're kind of nasty. They'll attack anybody who tries to come into their territory. Seriously, they're some of the bigger assholes of the bird world." He let the forward motion of the swing propel him to a standing position, one sweeping move that brought him straight in front of her. She didn't move, didn't breathe, as he brought his hands up to her cheeks. "But more importantly, Mindy, you were *never* the ugly duckling."

"I know, I know. I was the homecoming queen. But really only because of vote division. Honestly, it should have been Annalise Hernandez, but then she and Lisa Thibodeaux had that god-awful fight, and their boyfriends started smear-campaigning, and—"

"I remember, but that's not what I meant. It's that you always seemed to know where you belonged, and you always seemed to . . . I don't know, be so happy when you were making other people feel happy? I guess your parents had their issues, I'm sure that was a problem at home and maybe what I saw was only you compensating for that. But as far as school or the stables, or anywhere else you showed up . . . you were always so good at getting in there, being part of the group. Helping out, organizing things, being ten places at once. You kind of made things better wherever you went. This week you've made things better here. You're really *good* at that and you seem to enjoy it. It makes me sad to think you aren't getting that in Dallas." He stroked her jawline with his thumbs, pushed his fingertips into the hair behind her ears. Held her like she mattered. Like she was a precious thing he was afraid to drop.

She needed him to stop, or she was going to cry, and that wouldn't make things better for anything. It would have been so much easier if he'd been wrong. If he'd been an asshole. She reached up and squeezed his hands, then pulled away and made fists by her thighs to keep from reaching out for him again.

"I make things better at work. I'm good at my job. I've worked so hard to be good at it. Too hard to let myself get turned around by a bunch of emotional stuff I don't have time for."

The hurt on his face echoed in her gut. But what was she supposed to do? She wasn't wrong, she wasn't lying. She *had* worked hard to get where she was. This week's mammoth failure aside, she was good at what she did, and she had invested a huge amount of time and effort in her career. It wasn't smart to fuck that up just to get laid, no matter how brilliantly.

"I'll come there," he blurted.

Mindy's jaw literally dropped for a second before she could respond. "I had not even considered that possibility."

"I hadn't, either," he admitted. "But listen, it could work. I don't have a sub right now, you don't have a dom, neither of us is seeing anyone outside the lifestyle, either, right? And this week was great. We'd be stupid to just let it go. We can make it work. We can make *something* work."

Hope rose in her chest, seasoned with flattery and a sudden ridiculous affection. "We . . . could try?"

"Yes!"

The trail riders chose that moment to return, the whole group shouting and waving to them en route past the house to the barn. Mindy cleared her throat as she waved back, then turned to Logan, unsure what to say or how to feel. Too soon, too sudden.

"And maybe I could drive down sometimes, too. That seems only fair. Especially if the barn was free." She wanted to keep it on that footing, the D/s level. That seemed safer than suggesting they were trying to start up an actual . . . relationship.

Logan raised an eyebrow. "But we still get to go to the old drive-in."

"Okay. No scary movies, though," she bargained, sensing she'd already lost any hope of control over this thing between them. It was going wherever it was going, taking on a life of its own. "Because it's a huge abandoned field and we'd be there, unauthorized, after dark, and that seems like an open invitation to a hatchet murderer."

"You worry about murderers way too much."

"Maybe you don't worry about them enough," she suggested, looking past him toward the barn. "I should go help Lamar."

"Yeah, I need to help Robert, so . . ."

"I'll see you by the fire in a bit."

They hesitated, then moved in for an awkward hug that turned into something else halfway through. Not exactly friendly anymore, but not sexy, either. Something tender and new and too good to examine right then.

Mindy stepped away first and ran off the porch after the trail riders, her heart beating like a hummingbird's wings.

Stable duty turned out to be an easier task than she'd feared. It was cool enough outside, and it had been a slow enough ride, that none of the horses required much grooming. By sunset, she and Lamar were finished and headed back to the fire pit, where Logan greeted her with a plate of ribs and corn on the cob.

Hunger was the best sauce, not that the barbecue needed it. Like everything Robert had cooked that week, it was insanely good; the man was a genius in the kitchen and an artist over the grill.

She wondered if Logan would find more jobs for her to do before the evening was out. He seemed determined to fill every last minute of her remaining time, almost as if he could make her forget she wasn't really a part of the Hilltop crew. Or as if he himself kept forgetting that she didn't quite belong here.

She had trouble remembering that herself. When she'd finished her barbecue and stood by the fire pit chatting with the Jacksons, Bob made some corny joke and she laughed and caught Logan's eye and they'd shared a smile that was pure benign conspiracy. They both knew the joke was corny, but they both liked Bob because he seemed like a nice guy. That glance of pure understanding made her feel like they were suddenly in this thing together, Mindy and Logan. Partners in crime. It was an entirely novel, intoxicating way to feel about another person, and she had no idea what to do with it.

Logan caught her by the hand when he was ready to start the fire, positioning her next to him. "Okay, let's light this baby up. The inaugural run of the Hilltop Ranch fire pit." He lit the long fireplace match, touched it to the bundled newspaper in a few places, then tossed it into the gathering flames and stepped back, putting his arm around Mindy's shoulders.

Everybody clapped as the fire flickered and spread. When the applause died down, Mindy slowly slipped her arm around Logan's waist, giving him a subtle squeeze. When he looked down at her, she smiled back and hoped her expression told him she was proud of him. It had been a good week. He might not be able to make the ranch a going concern in the long run, but everybody'd had a good time, and that was worth something.

And maybe all hope wasn't lost, after all. There were always new ideas, new possibilities for him to try.

They could try. That was all they could do, but it seemed like enough.

The fire was really crackling when a crunch of boots on gravel caught Mindy's attention and she glanced off toward the path that led down to the cabins and the parking lot.

A balding, silver-haired man in a dark suit was approaching the fire, his features shadowed. He scanned the small crowd, his eyes finally landing on Mindy the moment he stepped close enough for her to recognize him.

She whispered, "Oh, it's . . ." at the same time Logan dropped his arm from her shoulders.

It was Bud Jameson.

Logan put his hand behind his back as he watched Jameson step into the ring of firelight, and he pinched himself hard. He was that convinced he must be having a nightmare.

His stomach tightened ominously around the rib dinner as Jameson reached out for Mindy, pulling her into a hug.

"How's my girl?"

She's not your fucking girl. Hot and pure and absolute, that was his first instinct, and he wanted to slam that truth into this asshole's face with his fist and lay him out cold with it. Mindy didn't reciprocate the hug; she stood stiffly and endured it, and Logan's only impulse was to get the guy off her.

But then the truth slammed back, worse than any punch. Of course she was Bud Jameson's girl. She had been all along. Had probably been reporting to Jameson the whole time.

Logan's skin started crawling, and he bit the inside of his cheek hard to keep from saying the first several things that popped into his mind after that realization.

"Mr. Hill!" Bud released Mindy and turned toward Logan. Mindy just stood where her stepfather had left her, staring down at the fire like the life had been sucked out of her. Possibly because her job was done now, and she didn't need to pretend anymore. What an exhausting fucking week it must have been for her.

Swallowing bile and barbecue sauce, Logan forced a grin and stuck his hand out to meet Bud's. "Mr. Jameson."

"Oh, call me Bud, call me Bud. Nice little hideaway you got here. Hope you don't mind my party-crashing." Jameson chuckled, looking around at the guests, who seemed puzzled by the visitor but willing enough to be charmed. "I was having dinner with a friend down in town and thought I'd stop by and check on Mindy. See how the vacation went."

Mindy turned around as though she realized some interaction would be appropriate. "Fine until now," she muttered, staring off toward the house.

It was obvious she couldn't wait to get away. Logan didn't blame her. He couldn't wait for her to get away, either.

"Oh, now," Jameson dismissed her. His folksy charm grated on Logan's nerves.

Robert and Diego started passing out marshmallows and long sticks, diverting the rest of the group's attention away from the tense scene playing out between Logan and Mindy and this new, too-friendly stranger. Chet shot Logan a questioning glance, but accepted a shrug-off—though he frowned and immediately fell into an equally tense conversation with Ethan.

Something pricked at Logan's mind—the fact that Jameson had even bothered with making a flimsy excuse for being in the neighborhood. "Dinner with a friend down in town?"

"Sure. Derek Larch."

The name sounded familiar . . . *Oh.* "My loan officer."

Jameson nodded, then shook his head with a heavy sigh. "You know, that boy has too much on his plate right now. And I told him, you know Derek, I've been in this business a long time. And when you have a heavy load, sometimes the only thing you can do is to pass along some of your riskier ventures." He lowered his voice, so the guests couldn't overhear, though he kept the same jovial tone. "Like bank loans you're afraid might be defaulted on, because the business concern doesn't seem too sound, and the proprietors have already been in for several talks about extending payment periods."

"*No,*" Mindy said.

Bud patted her arm. "Pumpkin, you've given this one a really good shot, and frankly done more than I could've ever asked for, but it's time for you to go roast some marshmallows and leave this to Pop and Mr. Hill to hash out. And text your mother, she'd like to hear from you."

Mindy's upper lip flexed, and the skin around her eyes went taut as she stared at her stepfather. She swallowed, and raised her balled fists to the level of her waist before lowering them along with her eyes.

In that few seconds, Logan would not have been surprised if Mindy had plucked one of the marshmallow sticks from the stack and skewered Bud Jameson in the heart with it. Then puked on his corpse, because she looked as ready to hurl as Logan felt. But then Logan remembered Mindy's role in all this. She might not like her stepfather, that much was clear, but the woman obviously knew which side her bread was buttered on.

Mindy exhaled, trembling with whatever emotion gripped her. When she spoke again, her voice was a rasp, a scoured whisper without hope. "I wasn't talking to you, Bud." Then she lifted her eyes to Logan's. "I didn't do this."

He couldn't answer her. His brain and mouth and heart didn't have enough organization to get out a coherent thought. After a moment she spun and walked away. Down the gravel path. Out of sight between the trees. Probably to her cabin. Possibly only to gather her bags and leave right that instant.

Now was not the time he could think about that.

"Sometime in the next few weeks, I propose we have a sit-down," Jameson said, pivoting slightly to take in the people, the fire, the silhouetted hills, the last scraps of red at the edge of the darkened sky. Everything Logan held dear and was probably about to lose. "We can still do this the easy way. I can make you a rich man. Trust me, sport, it's better than the hard way. You are not cut out for the hard way. And neither is that poor fella down at your pissant bank. You can keep what you have and enjoy it with some wells on it. Or I will own all this and I will fucking destroy you in the process."

"You—"

Jameson turned around and held up a hand. "Part of the easy way includes me pretending not to care whether you've been fucking my damn stepdaughter."

Enough. Logan closed his eyes, shook his head. He only had one more question in him. Anything else he'd have to deal with tomorrow. "Did she call you and tell you to come here after she'd softened me up enough? Was that the plan all along?"

Jameson snorted. "I'll be on my way, Logan. Expect some correspondence from Derek Larch and my office in the next few weeks. You have a good night now." Through some psychic power, or possibly just a business sense honed beyond anything Logan could have imagined possible, he craned his neck and nodded at Chet and Ethan.

"Y'all can come have your talk with our boy here now. We're all through."

He strolled off, smiling to the curious guests, and disappeared through the gap in the trees. Logan's hope that he would trip in the dark was dashed when a flashlight gleamed into life, then bounced out of sight down the hill.

Chapter Fourteen

Dallas was a nightmare.

It had always kind of been a nightmare. But before, Mindy had always been able to push that to the background, excuse it away based on circumstances. Of *course* she hated it. She'd had to move there after her parents' awful divorce, had to share a crappy apart-ment with her mom instead of moving into a dorm for college like she'd always expected she would. Then she'd had to work and study and worry . . . until her financial worry had been wiped out and re-placed with the fear that her mother had compromised herself for fi-nancial security with Bud Jameson.

Dallas was the place she'd lost her illusions, and told herself that was progress. The place she'd learned to talk about her hometown with a thin veneer of fondness over a thick base of scorn. Oh, Bolero . . . *bless its heart.*

She'd texted her mother from her cabin at Hilltop, only to learn there was some sort of surprise in store for her. A surprise at work. She'd find out Monday, Mom had told her. The texts practically vi-brated with ill-concealed excitement.

Bud was so tickled about it before he left for that conference in Houston. He was really upset he couldn't be there to tell you himself!

She had started to reply that she'd just seen Bud. That he'd just viciously crushed the dreams of a good man, then told her to run along and roast a goddamn marshmallow. But she didn't want to start saying things she'd regret, not when she was angry. Not when every fiber of her being wanted to march back up that hill and kick Bud Jameson in the nuts. She would find a way to broach the subject after she'd calmed down.

Monday morning at the office, she'd walked in to learn she'd scored that promotion after all. Just as her newly assigned assistant was peeling the cute wrapping paper off the shiny new nameplate outside her shiny new office—no more cubicle for Mindy—Bud texted her.

If I'd known how happy your mother would be about this, I'd have gone ahead and moved you up ages ago. This is for her.

Her new job was basically Bud's latest gift to her mom—just another tennis bracelet. He'd figured out a long time ago that his wife wasn't that rewarded by diamonds, but she was incredibly gratified when her only child did well and got another step closer to the financial security that she, Amelia Smith Valek Jameson, had spent so many years without.

It was diabolically clever. Mindy had to hand it to her stepfather. In order to decline the money, the job, the promotion, Mindy would have had to hurt her mother brutally. Bud knew she never would—and now she was caught in his web. A gilded cage.

By Tuesday, she'd already called a friend and made a date. And Wednesday night found her at the kink club, half-wishing she'd chosen any other activity for the evening.

"I'll use the waxed leather on you, but nothing harder," Miss Vixen had said once she saw Mindy naked.

"V, *please.*"

"No." The petite Dom had shaken her head firmly, black curls bobbing around her chin as she leaned over to drop her favorite tawse back into her toy bag. "Somebody beat me to it, girl. I'm not layering over all that, you'll end up with blood blisters or worse. You know that isn't my jam. Use common sense."

"Ugh. Fine."

"Can I get some damn respect, *please.*"

"Ma'am." It just didn't feel as good as *sir* at the moment. Especially not the *sirs* she'd laid on Logan when she was flying. "Sorry, Miss V. I'm just in a mood."

"You think? We could do a slapper. Lotta noise, at least. I have one other trick up my sleeve, too. I won't leave you hanging. Now let's . . . get you hanging."

So within a few minutes Mindy was naked under a scaffold, wrists cuffed and chained above her, body stretched so only her toes reached the ground. She did her best to let her mind float free as her partner laid into her with the flogger. Miss V tried to concentrate on the unmarked spots, but every so often she'd overlap one of the many lingering bruises and welts. Each time, Mindy winced with a flood of pain and accompanying emotions she didn't want to examine.

"Ten more," Miss V finally snapped at her. "Count 'em off!"

Mindy counted. It kept her in the pain, kept her from getting too spaced out, but she didn't want to feel *present*. She wanted to forget. When she got to ten, Miss V patted her on the ass. "Good girl. You need to relax, Ariel. You aren't singing for me tonight. You want to talk about it?"

"No, ma'am."

What was there to say, really? That she'd found the perfect Dom, perfect lover, possibly also a boyfriend rolled in there somewhere . . . then everything that had happened in her life up to that point had conspired to make their relationship impossible and fuck it all up? That just when she'd found somebody amazing, she'd realized she was doomed to be the instrument of his destruction? Too much to convey, even to V—who was also her friend Jamila, with whom she enjoyed shopping for overpriced shoes and binge-watching *Project Runway* on the rare weekend when neither of them was working or at the club.

V walked around in front of her, slapping the flogger into her free hand. "Is this about that dude ranch guy? What's his name, Landon? Logan?"

"V, come on."

"All right. Changing it up." V walked out of sight again, to rummage in her toy bag.

Whack! The slapper had more bark than bite, but Mindy would take it over conversation. She fell into the rhythm, sagging against the chains and closing her eyes, shutting out everything but the pain.

A lull came, and she wasn't expecting the next hit to be on the front. A sharp *crack* to the top of one thigh, forcing her eyes wide open. V chuckled. "That woke you up."

"Evil."

"Mm-hmm."

V didn't *look* evil. She looked kind of like Glinda the Good Witch some nights, but tonight it was more jewelry box ballerina. Pale pink tutu, pale pink brocade corset, pink toe shoe–inspired stilettos. Her dark skin and hair were a startling contrast to the outfit, as always—

she favored icy pinks, blues, and pure whites, and she loved the attention her look earned her. Except when new Doms to the local scene mistook her for a submissive. Then her head exploded while she set them straight.

She was the best kind of evil, though. The kind with a heart. She popped the slapper across one of Mindy's nipples, then the other, alternated between them a few times, then smacked the noisy leather strap without warning against the still-flowering bite-mark bruise. Mindy cried out, needing more. V obliged with one more slap at the spot before disappearing again.

This time, she came back with the evil stick. Concentrated doses of sting, carefully targeted to all the bare spots V could find. The outer thighs, a few safe zones on Mindy's lower back and mid-torso.

When V grazed the slender, springy rod over the bite mark, moving her other hand in preparation to pull it back for a strike, Mindy shook her head, surprising even herself. "No, don't."

She kept aiming, pulling back on the stick.

"Red."

V jerked her hand away, clearly startled, and caught herself on the chin with the edge of the stick. "Ow! Fuck!"

"Oh no! Are you okay?" Mindy rattled the chains, but she didn't have enough slack to get herself free without a lot of effort.

"Yeah, I'm fine." V tossed the stick down next to her back and stepped to the side of the scaffold, grabbing a folding step stool. She propped it next to Mindy and climbed up to unhook the safety clips. "Are *you* okay? You've never safed out on me before. Did I fuck up?"

"Oh, God no." Mindy hugged V, taking advantage of the stool while V was on it. Usually Mindy was taller, but she knew V enjoyed the illusion of height. "You were great. I'm just not in the right headspace today. I'm sorry, I should have suggested dumb movie night instead."

"I was worried I'd really hurt something on one of those overworked spots. I *told* you. You should listen to me, I'm a doctor."

"I know, I know. I'm sorry."

"Just glad you're okay."

They cuddled for a minute, reassuring one another, then signed off the hug with "*let's wrap this up*" pats.

V wobbled off the stool. "To be honest, dumb movie night probably wouldn't have gotten me out of the house. I think you need to talk, though. You wanna go out to the lounge?"

The club wasn't a huge space, and the lounge was even smaller. Bodies would be jostling together, many of them funky after vigorous scenes. Claustrophobic.

"I wish we could go somewhere outside."

V zipped her bag and slung it over her shoulder. "Yeah, I wish that, too, but neither of us is dressed for it. I drove here in this. Your tits are hanging out of that shirt if anybody looks close."

Mindy fingered the light jersey of the sleeveless yoga shirt she liked to throw on after a scene. It was comfortable and didn't press on any welts while she drove home, but without a sports bra under it, it was a public indecency citation waiting to happen. "What we need is a kink venue with a ton of open space, and a hotel right there so people can spend the night if they're too loopy to drive home after a scene."

In her mind, a bell chimed, and an image sprang to life. Later, she would always recall that the idea literally came to her with the clear, sweet tone of a single church bell.

"Oh my God," she said. "V, I know what Logan can do to turn a quick profit at the ranch."

"What?" The bell chimed again, and V pulled her phone from the pocket of her bag and checked the screen. "Hang on, gotta look at this. I may need to call back." She was already wending her way toward the door to the lounge. She couldn't speak on the phone inside the playroom—though an exception would have probably been made for her, if she'd explained it was work-related. V was a clinical cardiologist, and she was almost never *not* in touch with her office staff.

Mindy followed V at a more leisurely place, feeling better than she had since she'd seen her stepfather walk up to Logan at the fire pit over a week earlier. The fact that the bell had actually been V's new message tone mattered not at all. Mindy'd had a vision, and she finally knew how to help Logan. Now all she had to do was convince him to trust her.

Easy-peasy.

"Well, she's fucking nuts."

Logan nodded sadly at his brother and continued typing in his listing information. "Should we start the description with the distance from San Antonio or Austin, do you think? Having both seems too wordy."

"San Antonio," Ethan replied with a wave of his hand. "Sounds more old-time Texas-style. People coming from inside the state will know where it is, anyway. You're just trying to pull Yankees."

Logan sighed and backspaced, changing the first sentence for the tenth time. He wanted to be done with this, so he could get some sleep, so he could have some sort of energy tomorrow when he talked to that weekend's too-small group of guests. It was hard to razzle-dazzle folks when he was barely able to keep his eyes open. "Once we hit Send on this, we have maybe two weeks to clean out the main house. Assuming anybody wants to rent."

"Put in something like *ideal writing retreat*. Talk about the view." Ethan stalked across the office, still staring at the email Logan had forwarded him. "Absolutely fucking psycho wacko nutballs."

"Gee, Ev, don't hold back . . ." Logan hadn't actually decided quite how to feel about Mindy. Or the fact that she'd emailed him—since he hadn't accepted her calls. Or the idea she'd proposed in that email.

"This is what happens when you put your dick in evil."

Logan stood, shoving the rolling chair back so hard it hit the far wall. "*Dude.*"

His little brother's eyes went wide. "Is that not where we were with this?"

"I don't *know.*"

"Fuck." Ethan slipped his phone back his pocket and laced his hands behind his neck. "Sorry, man. I thought that was—I'm really sorry."

Sighing, Logan retrieved his chair and flopped back into it. "You didn't see her face when he talked to her. Or when she claimed she didn't do it. I'm pissed as fucking hell and I'm sick about the whole situation, but I do not know what to believe about her right now. Whether she was reporting back to fucking Bud Jameson the whole time, or looking at my spreadsheets and distracting me while Bud figured out the bank thing, or called him out to close the deal or what." And he couldn't stand to hear anybody bashing her until he knew it was justified. Things had been so much simpler when his biggest frustration was that he couldn't parade Mindy across the stable yard naked on a leash . . .

Huh.

"Do you want me to write the description thing, so you can get some sleep? You look wrecked." Ethan leaned over the keyboard. Logan hardly noticed him.

A sudden vision danced before his eyes with the strength of a hallucination. Mindy, in just a collar and a pain-face, suspended from the rafters in the old barn. Other subs disporting themselves around the hay bales. Doms strolling across the lawn, finding wide-open spaces to throw bullwhips. A pony derby . . . taking place in an actual corral. Kink *rodeo.*

"We'd have to make the horse barn strictly off-limits . . ." he murmured. "And find some way to keep Lamar away."

"What? He'll be up like usual to take care of the horses. Renting out the main house won't change that. You'll just be down in the cabins, you can police the horse barn during the day. Do we need to get you some better Wi-Fi down there, by the way?" Ethan started typing.

"It wouldn't even have to be every weekend, we could do it like a mini-convention once a month or something." Logan sat up and tapped Ethan's shoulder, trying to nudge him away from the computer. "Charge for the weekend or just the day, people could wear those wristbands. We already know the sheriff isn't gonna raid the place, right? He'll be up here playing as soon as he's off-duty."

Ethan finally stepped aside, staring at him like he was spouting gibberish. "What the hell are you *talking* about?"

Logan was already typing, pulling up his profile on KinkBook, looking at his notifications. "People in my feed were complaining this week because some meet-up in San Antonio got cancelled. It was supposed to be two weekends from now. We'd have two full weeks to set up an alternative. If we started posting information now—"

"Wait, what the *hell*? Are you talking about Mindy's idea? Her batshit-crazy idea?"

By way of response, Logan clicked the link to the original event, navigated to the registration page, and pointed to the fee. "That was a single-day event with a play party at night. Just out of people I knew from Houston, over a dozen people were planning to make the trip. Those were the ones I knew were *actually* going to go. They'd paid up-front. That fee doesn't include the cost of the hotel room or meals."

Ethan made a skeptical noise then did a double-take at the screen, studied the page for a few seconds, obviously doing the math in his head. "It says the event is capped at a hundred fifty people. So that would mean . . . Holy shit. I've been to those but I never thought about . . . holy shit."

"Right? I mean we don't have a place to put more than a dozen right now. Maybe twenty if we're at full capacity and clear a few rooms in the main house, but—"

"Camping. Kinky campout."

They looked at each other. Logan turned the idea over a few times. "We'd have to clear out the old site. Relight the walking trail and fill some potholes on the back road. Get the septic truck up there to deal with the johns. Ew, and probably an exterminator, I hate to think what—"

"Maybe see if it's cheaper to rent some Porta-Johns at first."

"Chet would know, he has to deal with all that crap when the bikers have the rally."

Ethan snickered. "All that crap."

"Heh. But seriously, even if we only got a few dozen people and charged the off-season rate, that would still be a full house in cabins plus the campers at, what . . . twenty bucks a head per night? For two nights. Plus that cover charge for the event. That's . . . wow. *Wow.* We could get caught up on the bills, get a little ahead with the bank. Go in to the next regular weekend in the black instead of already in the red. We'd at least have some kind of bargaining position with Derek. Jesus, Ethan, this could *work*."

"I'm gonna call Chet." Ethan took his phone out, then cursed. "Fuck, no, I'm gonna go to sleep, and so should you, because it's already one o'clock on Sunday morning and you need to be Mister Chipper Host for your vanilla guests at breakfast. But after I wake up, I'll call Chet and talk to Robert and Diego. Thank God you picked kinky friends to hire, that's gonna make this so much easier. So, tomorrow you focus on making sure everybody gets fed and trail-ridden then packed and gone with smiles on their faces. And then you know what you need to do, right?"

Logan groaned. He did know. That didn't mean he had to look forward to it.

Except that part of him *did* look forward to it. The part that never wanted to talk to her again and the part that wanted to see her *right now* were having a slap fight in his head. Feelings were hard. "I have to call Mindy."

If this is some sort of trick . . .

If you're planning to set up some sort of scandal . . .

If your intention is to get people here then threaten to doxx them . . .

All valid concerns, and Mindy knew why Logan voiced them. But that didn't mean they didn't hurt. So much more than anything he'd ever done to her with a flogger, or a bullwhip, or a cane, or his perfect, perfect teeth.

"I understand," she said, when what she meant was, *It's so good to hear your voice again.* "I'll be the safeguard. I'll be there myself. Naked the whole time, if that's what it takes."

Logan coughed, a harsh note over the iffy cell connection. "You'd like that, wouldn't you?"

"Well . . . yeah, kinda." She squirmed in her too-soft executive leather chair. The office was as quiet as a tomb; she always felt too loud when she spoke on the phone in there, but never more so than when Logan Hill was making her think about strolling across his ranch naked. "Especially if I had a collar on."

"Don't push your luck, Mindy."

"Right. Sorry, sir."

She'd hit Send on her email on Friday night. He hadn't called her until Monday morning. It had been the longest weekend of her life, following the longest week of her life. When she'd seen his number on her screen, she'd almost passed out from anticipation. And when she'd realized he wasn't calling to yell at her, but to tell her he was running with her idea . . .

She put her head down on the desk, anchoring the phone between her ear and the mahogany. She didn't know where Bud had come up with the office furniture, but it was all beautiful. Not Mindy's taste— her mom's. She wondered if he'd let Amelia decorate the office as part of the surprise.

"You're on KinkBook, right?" Logan asked. "Do you have

friends in Dallas who were planning to go to the MiniKinkFest two weeks from now?"

"They canceled it," she mumbled. "Everybody was so pissed. My friend Jam—Miss Vixen only gets about one weekend off a century. That was her big plan. And all her fangirls and fanboys were probably going to follow her down there."

"There was a fire at their venue."

"I know, but it was still disappointing." Why did he care so much about the cancelled MiniKinkFest anyway?

"Can you get on KinkBook or do whatever you do, and get those folks to sign up to come to the ranch instead that weekend? It's short notice, but there's this existing pool of people who'd made plans."

"Oh my God." She sat up, flipping the phone to the desk; she fumbled to recover it. "That's *brilliant*. Where will you put everyone, though? The main house rooms aren't ready, the cabins won't hold nearly that many people, and there's no way the kitchen could handle that kind of capacity, even if Robert had half a dozen helpers."

"We probably won't get very many people, even with the cancellation." Logan sounded excited nevertheless. "But we think we can do maybe two dozen if we get the campsite cleared out. Remember, we passed that area on the low trail rides? It's not even a hundred yards from the house as the crow flies, the riding trail just takes a roundabout way to get there. There's a straight-shot trail buried in grass and shrubs. Robert and Diego are helping me find that later today. Used to be gravel, but it's probably mostly dirt now. Eventually we'll want maybe some compacted pea gravel or something easy on bare feet. Not that bare feet are a great idea in the hill country in the dark, but you know, people aren't going to want their subs in boots, and a lot of folks will want to be in heels. So just thinking ahead."

"Making sure the horse barn is off-limits is important, too."

"Already on it." He sighed into the phone, causing more noise overload. "So, how are you?"

Awful. "Oh, I'm fine. How are *you*?"

"I am also fine."

If she didn't keep him talking, the call would be over soon. "I got a promotion? But it's . . . weird."

"Hmm. Weird how?"

"Well. It's a bigger title than I asked for. And a lot more money.

But I don't actually have any authority." She flicked her gaze around the office nervously as if people might be listening in at the door or windows. "I'm basically the best-paid rubber-stamp wielder in the city now. Supposedly I jumped up a step and now supervise a bunch of landmen. But literally all I do is receive their reports and contracts, read them, sign off that I've read them, and forward them up the food chain. That's it."

Some rustling noises came over the line; it sounded like Logan was either outside in the wind, or doing something with his hands. "Okay. That is weird. That doesn't sound like a real job."

"I don't think it is. I think he just wanted to get me out of the way and make my mom happy by giving me more shopping money and free time. And I hate it. And I hate him." Saying it out loud was such a relief she nearly cried. "And, Logan, he keeps making these digs about his friends at your bank, and playing golf with Derek Larch's father-in-law. I think he's planning something. More of something, I mean. Something specific." She'd tried to ask around surreptitiously, but had gotten nowhere. Only her assistant, Terry, talked to her anymore, and that was mostly wondering when the actual work would start.

Never, she was tempted to say. *You may feel free to play computer games and shop online all day long.* She made assignments up instead. So far, Terry seemed happy enough with the busywork. Eventually, though, Mindy would run out of tasks. For her part, she resisted the urge to change her spending habits. She kept nursing along her clunker of a car. She avoided the truly outrageously expensive shoes. She put the infusion of extra cash straight into savings. Just in case.

"Can you tell me anything in particular?"

"Not yet. I'm not being cagey, I just don't know anything." She sighed and plunked her head down again. "Tell me what I can do to help you get ready for the big event. Please give me something to do."

He laughed. A miraculous sound, a rainbow after a storm. "A job where you're not helping anybody, and you've been doing that for a whole week? Okay, you've been tortured enough. I'll send you a link to the shared to-do list, you can pick whatever strikes your fancy."

"Really?"

"Yes, really."

"Oh my God, *thank you*."

Logan laughed again, then the golden sound tapered off into a sigh. "And you'll be here next Friday by no later than four in the afternoon, right? To help greet people and get their paperwork signed and all that?"

"Three thirty sharp," she promised. "I won't even go in to work that morning. I'll leave straight from home. Since apparently I'm also on a flex schedule now."

"Okay then. I'll see you a week from Friday. And talk to you before then, I guess."

It would have to do. "Got it, sir."

"Get to work."

"Giddyup!"

"Wait . . . say that again."

"Giddyup?"

He whooped, and Mindy held the phone out from her ear for a second until it seemed safe. She could hear jostling, air rushing past, as if he was running with the phone. And then, slightly muffled, "Giddyup! There's your name!"

"Oh . . . oooh," said somebody wherever Logan was calling from. "Yeah, that could work. I'll update the thing. That's good. Nice work, bro."

"No, not me." He breathed into the phone again. "Nice work, Mindy."

She'd named the event, apparently. Which made her feel ten times more responsible for the outcome. But it was good to feel responsible for something. "Thank you."

"And I'll see you a week from Friday."

"You will."

"Okay. Well, 'bye for now."

Oh God. It was bad high school dating. Hopefully they wouldn't get stuck in a good-bye loop. "Okay. 'Bye."

"Later."

She didn't reply; she was strong and ended the call before she could say anything stupid. End on a high note, that was always the best plan.

Mindy allowed herself a slow count of ten to do nothing but breathe. Then she slid her personal laptop out of her briefcase, booted it up, and got to work.

Chapter Fifteen

Planning a last-minute weekend gathering for a few dozen kink-sters, complete with camping, barbecue, and a "rodeo" feature event, turned out to be like playing organizational whack-a-mole. Drunk. While attempting to win at chess.

Solving one problem created ten more little problems. Any one of which might blossom with unseen ramifications. And that was even ignoring the baseline issues of legality and privacy, which Chet was always willing to bring up just when things seemed to be calming down.

"I cannot recommend hiring off-duty officers or deputies to secure entrances and exits. Even the kink-aware."

Ethan had clapped him on the shoulder. "Got it covered, cuz. Bikers."

"I beg your pardon?"

"*Bikers*. Well, not real bikers, I don't think? A bunch of 'motor-cycle enthusiasts'"—Ethan air-quoted the term—"who are also members of the club in San Antonio that was organizing the Mini-KinkFest. They usually all take shifts as dungeon masters at MKF and a bunch of local clubs. Plus, they love Bolero, they come every year for the bike rally. And when they found out about Giddyup they volunteered to help with the entrance security in rotations if they can get half off on admission and we waive the camping fee. The beauti-ful part is, two of them have big RVs, and they plan to park at the KOA down the road and bike in and out from there. We won't even have to house them."

Chet had frowned and said, "I'll require their bonafides." But ap-parently he'd been satisfied by whatever he'd learned, because that was the last Logan had heard of it.

Calculating the optimal number of portable toilets to reserve when the crowd size kept growing led to a few conversations that were as frustrating as they were disgusting. Robert finally stepped between Logan and Ethan when their verbal shit-slinging started heading down memory lane and the whole scene got too heated for him to take.

"*Boss*. And baby boss."

Ethan had given him the side-eye. "Never."

"If I take this over and promise to have enough crappers there on the day, will you both promise to stop talking about this, *please*? Because this shit ain't healthy."

"People pissing out behind the house when Mom isn't looking is what's not healthy, *Ethan*." Logan had seethed.

"I was *four*."

"You were old enough to throw me under the bus and say I made you do it. *Multiple times*."

But they'd eventually let it go, and Robert had gotten them to shake on the agreement to *never talk about portable toilets again*.

Mindy had been Skyped in when the food problem was discussed, and Diego had fretted about having time to construct a platform in the old barn and some seating for a shibari demo. Logan had also been bemoaning the lack of temporary stalls for staging the ponies at the rodeo/derby.

Ethan had cracked up when he realized Logan was worried about it. "Dude . . . and you didn't ask the *large animal vet* with a practice thirty-five minutes away? I already marked the stalls off on the spreadsheet, didn't you *check*?"

Then Chet had pointed out that he had a year's worth of perfectly fine venison already butchered and stored in his deep freeze that he was willing to donate for at least one evening's feast. "It would make an excellent hearty stew."

Mindy had said, "Oh God. Y'all. This is . . . you know, that old movie, with Mickey Rooney and Judy Garland? Except instead of making costumes, it's, 'My cousin has some deer meat we can use for stew.' 'My brother knows how to make stalls for human horses.' 'My grandpa has an old barn where we can make a stage.'"

And in unison, they'd all shouted, "Hey, kids! Let's put on a show!"

Logan kept the Skype connection open after the others left his office, reluctant to let Mindy out of his sight. She was patched in from home, it looked like—she was wearing a Mickey Mouse T-shirt and seemed to be sitting on a couch or large chair of some deep red velvet or suede. The bottom edge of a painting was visible behind her head at the top of the camera frame. Abstract art in warm tones . . . or possibly the limited view only made it seem abstract.

With her strawberry hair against the reds, browns, and golds, it was like looking at a fire. Or possibly the warmth Logan perceived had nothing to do with the visuals.

"So how's the non-job going? Still . . . non?"

She shrugged. "The other day I got called in to a meeting with Bud and some of the landmen who theoretically report to me. I didn't get a word in the entire time. I guess I'm just lucky they weren't asking me to get them coffee. And after the other guys finished up and cleared out, Bud gave me this look like, what was I still doing there? I asked him why I even needed to be at the meeting, since it was clear he'd just made me into a useless middleman and didn't trust me with any real work."

"Whoa." Logan knew just enough about Mindy's relationship with her stepfather to know she didn't normally voice those concerns out loud. "What did he say?"

She sighed. "Stuff about my mom being happy. And how I should be grateful that I was basically living like one of the characters on *Dallas*—the TV show, you know, how they all worked for Ewing Oil or whatever but nobody ever seemed to do any actual work. That this way he didn't *have* to worry about me or my 'oddly placed loyalties.' And then he said my car was a disgrace to upper management and I really should replace it as soon as possible because he had an image to maintain and I was part of that image."

Logan had seen Mindy's car and privately agreed it should be replaced, for safety if for no other reason, but he wisely kept that to himself. "Loyalty to who?"

She ran her hands through her hair, letting the strands fall back in disarray. "I may have said something about big corporate greed and how small business was supposed to be the American way and people should be able to make their own choices about what to do with their assets, free from coercion. Blah, blah, blah, ethics in business, blah."

Me. Loyalty to me. "You know, I . . . owe you an apology." He leaned closer to the computer as if that meant anything over video, then realized it only made his face huge from her perspective, so then he sat back in his chair as Mindy's face screwed up in puzzlement. "You were telling the truth. After those first few hours, you came clean about why you were here, and . . . you told the truth after that. And I'm sorry I believed you were still in cahoots with Bud that whole time. That the whole thing was some kind of honey trap."

She bit her lip, then sucked it out with a popping noise. "Well. You had every reason. I mean, there he was. And I was so flustered I couldn't even say much. I have this . . . *thing* with authority figures, you know?"

Logan laughed. "Uh, yeah. I got that."

"I should have stuck around and stuck up for myself instead of running away. Or quit my job right then."

"I'd have hired you on the spot." He didn't know where it came from, but it felt right. Having her at the ranch full-time. She would be nothing but helpful. It would make good business sense somehow.

Mindy cocked her head. "With what part of your currently nonexistent budget, Math Man? For an engineer you sure can lie to yourself about numbers."

"Okay," he admitted, "maybe not on the spot. But . . . sometime? If Giddyup is a success?"

The look she gave him was half-flirting, half-pitying. "Dude. Do you even want to know my current salary? I'm not going to say I'm all about the money, but it is a *considerable* amount of money. And my mom is *so* thrilled. She'd be devastated if I left under a cloud. And I still think there's a chance if I suck it up for a little while, Bud will finally give me some stuff to do." She clenched her jaw, suddenly looking determined. Logan wasn't sure who she was trying to convince, him or herself. "He knows I'm capable. I think the situation right now is just his weird way of punishing me for going AWOL, trying to get the deal with you, and . . . well, failing. And sleeping with you instead. Eventually he's got to let me do some work for all this compensation. He's a businessman. He's not going to keep paying this much just to show me he has me under his thumb, right?"

Logan considered it a moment, then shrugged. "You know him better."

"Yeah. That's what I'm afraid of."

"There's a place for you here," he insisted gently.

She looked away from the camera. "On the ranch, you mean? Or . . ."

Logan wasn't sure how to separate the two. The ranch was his life now; he only knew that Mindy fit in somehow. He hadn't felt complete since she'd left. "We could figure that out as we went along, maybe?"

"That's a lot of uncertainty for such a tall order." She looked back at him, a softer smile curving her lips. Gentle, but a little sad. "I guess we can talk about it when I get there next Friday."

"Fair enough." He didn't want to let her go yet. "You could just come as an attendee, too. I don't want to be just another guy trying to put you to work. I mean, I'll be busy during the event, but you said you had friends who were coming, so I guess you could still play with—"

She laughed. "I said I'd be there, Logan. It's okay. You don't have to offer further inducements."

They did the awkward, too-long, you-first good-bye thing again, then signed off; Logan wished after the fact that he'd thought to screenshot Mindy's face. Then he realized that was potentially kind of creepy, or at least overly lovesick, and he was not aiming to be either of those things.

If only he could offer her an inducement the size of the fat paycheck and maternal satisfaction she was getting from Bud Jameson. Logan knew it wasn't exactly a direct competition, but it was still hard to think how to woo her away from that lifestyle.

Was that what he was doing now? Trying to woo her? He put the thought aside and tried to focus on the upcoming event.

All in all, Logan couldn't complain. The problems got sorted out. The laughs outnumbered the headaches. Giddyup sold out and the waiting list was longer than the list of attendees.

On the other hand, Derek Larch kept calling and emailing him. Putting more pressure on, implying more and more strongly that it really wasn't up to Derek anymore. His superiors at the bank's HQ were demanding he tighten up. Get rid of the risks, clamp down on the late pays. He'd done as much as he could, Derek implied strongly . . . and Logan really should have taken Bud Jameson's offer to meet and talk instead of telling him to go piss up a rope.

It had been pretty damn satisfying to tell him that, though.

When that Friday finally dawned, he walked outside and thanked the weather gods. Early April could have gone any direction, from cold and rainy to blazing heat and drought. But it was cool and fair and not too humid, and Logan felt something stir inside him as he sipped his coffee and watched the sunrise. Hope. For the first time in months, Logan actually had hope.

The staff would be filtering in as they finished up their other jobs. Chet couldn't make it until late in the evening, but Ethan would be there after lunch sometime. And at three thirty sharp, Logan would get to see Mindy again. He fingered the length of fine cord in his pocket, then tried to clear his mind. He still had a spreadsheet full of last-minute details to see to and smooth out and check off. More than enough to keep him busy.

At lunchtime, Logan had trouble forcing down his second ham sandwich, but he muscled through it. He wanted to be well fortified. He didn't want to think about seeing Mindy again. He was worried if he started, if he let that thought and the attendant hope and want into his mind, he'd lose sight of all the myriad things he was supposed to keep track of for the weekend. All the things everybody was counting on him to do.

Monday they would know whether the profit was real—whether the risk had been worth it. For the weekend, all they could do was stick to the plan as much as possible, roll with any last-minute changes, and try to make sure everybody had a great time without getting hurt . . . in unintended ways.

The arrival of Ethan and the biker security crew kept him occupied for some time after lunch. A great group of folks, eight bearded guys and four "old ladies" who rolled their eyes when their husbands referred to them that way . . . they invited Logan over to the campground to visit and have cookies any time he liked while they were there.

"Bikes have always been Gerry's hobby," one of them, Judy, explained with a sweet, almost maternal smile. Then she winked and whispered, "He's really a tax accountant. I am, too, that's how we met. I'm the one who got him into kink, that was always *my* hobby."

The group also contained, it turned out, a few fellow engineers, several IT folks, a high school math teacher, and a lawyer.

Ethan beamed with pride as he and Logan helped the first shift of two guards set up the checkpoint across the main road. There was already a gate at the cattle guard, right below the spot where the main drive forked off into the smaller road leading directly to the campsite. The gate was usually propped open; the bikers closed it, then set up a portable sunshade with a camp table and chairs right next to the big folding sign that read, "Welcome to GIDDYUP! (Private event: no general admission)." Then the "security team" settled in with the final checklist, a walkie-talkie, and a chart detailing who would be taking the subsequent shifts. They had everything covered.

"Aren't these guys *awesome*?" Ethan stage-whispered to Logan as they unloaded an ice chest with water bottles, sodas, and snacks from the back of Logan's truck.

"They do look intimidating," Logan agreed. Even knowing that Big Gerry and "Bloodworm" were an accountant and a sys admin, respectively, he was a bit daunted by their beards and leathers and overall air of badassery. "And everyone will totally buy that the private function is a biker thing, too. That was a stroke of genius."

They lugged the cooler under the shade tent; Ethan grunted as he lowered his side. "They'll probably wonder why it isn't louder, but that can be part of the mystique, I guess."

"I am a little worried one of Chet's deputies might miss a memo and try to hassle these guys."

"Logan. Chill. Things will be *fine*."

"Yeah, but," he suggested, "what if they *aren't*? This whole thing is still kind of crazy, and if it goes wrong, the potential for disaster is *huge*. I'm on board, but that doesn't mean it's not sane to worry."

Ethan opened the cooler and selected a water bottle, twisting the top off and emptying a third of it in one gulp, then wiping his mouth on his sleeve. "You're a naysayer."

Logan closed the cooler firmly. "I'm not a naysayer."

"You just said . . . that was just naysaying, what you just said. You're being one *right now*."

"So anybody who harbors a reasonable concern is a—who *says* that, anyway? Nobody calls people naysayers anymore, this isn't the freaking eighteen-nineties, Ethan."

His brother grinned. "Reckon I'll call folks what I want to call folks, dagnabbit." He pretended to hawk and spit, making a *ptooie* sound as if he'd slung chaw at a spittoon.

"It's really a shame you're too late for the vaudeville circuit."

Bloodworm reached past them to open the cooler and pull out a Dr Pepper. "Ah, brotherly love. Change of subject, Doc, but after our shift here, you're gonna help me tie up Mrs. Bloodworm, right?"

Ethan nodded. "I am, indeed, if she's still interested. I cheated and blocked out a ten o'clock slot on the sign-up sheet in the old barn. On one of the side beams. That'll give you plenty of time to get some dinner, shower, whatever."

"Perfect."

Logan checked the time. Two o'clock. Details flooded his brain, and he bounced on his toes, trying to drive some of the stress out.

A car drove up, the driver's window rolling down as it slowed to a stop. Logan vaguely recognized the driver from his usual club in Houston, and waved a greeting as Bloodworm checked him off a list and Big Gerry let him through the gate, directing him up the camp-site driveway. A couple of volunteers from the MiniKinkFest planning group, who'd arrived an hour or so earlier, would help him out from there, getting him to his assigned parking spot and tent pad.

A truck with a trailer in tow pulled into the spot the car had just vacated.

Logan snagged the walkie-talkie and gave Diego and Robert the heads-up that their guests were starting to arrive.

A wasp nest was reported on the side of one of the rented Porta-Johns. Logan investigated, found it was just dirt daubers, but knocked the mud nests off anyway.

A dead snake was found near one of the tent pads. But it was dead, and it was just a small brown grass snake, so it wasn't a big deal.

Robert broke down in tears when he thought he'd ruined one of the giant pots of slow-simmering venison stew with too much salt. But he pulled himself together, threw a few extra potatoes into the mix, and soon pronounced it fit to serve to dignitaries and heads of state. Logan assured him that if he ran across any heads of state, he'd send them straight up to the buffet line at supper time.

Logan kept his phone firmly in his pocket. He had been good all day—all two weeks, really—trying to play it cool. Not make any as-sumptions about Mindy's plans once she arrived at the ranch. To say they hadn't parted on good terms was the understatement of the cen-tury, and no definitive plans had been made on their subsequent calls and Skypes, so he had no idea what would happen during the Big

Kinky Weekend of Kinkiness; he just thought it was a good sign she'd planned to attend. A show of good faith, and a guarantee, as she herself had pointed out. She could hardly point a finger at anybody else if she was there, too, getting her freak on. Naked. Hopefully.

He told himself she could get her freak on with any number of people; there would almost certainly be volunteers to help her with that. It was wrong to want to kick those volunteers out of line and demand she let only Logan play with her. They were both adults. They could have a professional relationship. They could even let bygones be bygones, and just be old friends who knew each other from way back. It didn't have to *mean* anything.

At three o'clock he texted her. Knowing she was driving and probably couldn't reply, knowing she was likely only half an hour away at most anyway, it was only a smiley-face emoji. Let her take it as she would.

Half an hour later, his phone buzzed in his pocket.

She'd replied with a sad face.

He was still puzzling over it when his walkie-talkie hissed at him. The security gate's channel. He toggled the switch, icy fear seeping from his heart to chill his veins. "Logan."

"Boss? Yeah, I think you need to get down here. We have a problem."

From the moment Mindy's day had started, it had been heading downhill. She should have never gotten out of bed. No, she should have never checked her email after waking up, that was really the turning point.

Or maybe it was deciding not to replace her car when she got the raise. Another possibility.

She refused to draw the self-blame line back any further. She wouldn't say she should have never gone to Hilltop Ranch in the first place. And she wouldn't say she should have never helped plan this so-crazy-it-just-might-work weekend to help Logan save the place.

Although those choices certainly hadn't made her current life any easier.

That morning's nine o'clock meeting, called at the last minute via email, had been the final nail in the coffin of her career hopes. Bud and her assistant had both known she was planning to go out of town that morning, so she'd assumed the meeting had to be an emergency;

she'd thought, foolishly as it turned out, that she might even be needed at the office for her expertise.

When she'd dashed into the conference room at nine fifteen, hair still slightly damp, wearing a too-warm blazer to hide the fact that her wrinkled dress needed a visit to the dry cleaner, she'd pulled up short at the sight of Bud, two of Mindy's "team" members, and her assistant, clearing the agendas from the table and gathering up their coffee cups.

"Oh, we're done, Mindy," Terry had said perkily. "Didn't you get the follow-up email?"

"We didn't need you for this one after all," one of the land men added. "Sometimes faster to cut out the middleman." He seemed to realize what he'd said, after his mouth was closed. He ducked his head and sped from the room, mumbling something about a call he needed to make.

Bud hadn't said anything until the rest of them left. Then he'd smiled his most pleasant, avuncular smile before speaking. "Taking a trip over your long weekend, right?"

"Yep." And she could have been on the road already. "Did you really get me in here for nothing?"

"Oh no." His smile turned nasty. "I just wanted to remind you, before your little junket, that you dance to my tune now. Have a nice drive, ballerina."

Then he'd nodded at her and gone on his way. He hadn't needed to say anything more to make his point; he controlled her. He'd orchestrated the whole meeting to rub her face in that fact.

She'd gone to her office, closed the door, and sat for at least twenty minutes, willing tears of anger and frustration not to fall. She'd fingered her cell phone, fighting the temptation to text Logan. She didn't need to look outside for sympathy; she needed to quit her job and let her mother know what a conniving tool she'd married.

Her mother would not want to believe that of Bud. And Mindy might fuck up their relationship permanently. But she'd been silent long enough.

Monday, she'd finally decided. She would quit and talk to her mom on Monday, after a weekend of stress relief. Or at least of a different flavor of stress.

Then she'd gotten into her car, not bothering to change because she was starting the drive so much later than she'd expected. She could change at Hilltop.

The noises had started right outside Waco, after she'd stopped for gas. The noises, and the slight shiver of the steering wheel. An alignment problem, possibly. She turned the radio up a notch louder and ignored it. Sang along to all the classic country she could find, tuning the radio occasionally as local stations faded in and out of range.

Up until the outskirts of Bolero, she did a great job of fooling herself that the rattling wasn't getting any worse. But the second she hit the intersection to turn either toward town or up toward the hills, and tried to make the turn, the steering wheel shimmied so hard she could hardly grip it. Straight ahead one mile or so was a gas station at the edge of town. Instead of turning, she headed for that instead, checking the time on her phone and noticing she'd missed a text.

It was nearly three thirty. The text was a smiley face from Logan from a half hour earlier.

The wheel shook again and she tossed the phone back into the passenger seat, using both hands to guide it down the road. She could see the gas station up ahead.

A horrible ratcheting noise filled the car, and she yanked the wheel to one side, steering sharply for the shoulder. Something caught and scraped against the pavement, as if the car was dragging some piece of machinery along under it. The noise ended in a heavy, metallic *clunk* as the car shuddered to a halt.

Heart pounding, Mindy turned the ignition off and gasped for air; until then, she hadn't realized that it wasn't just the car shaking, it was *her*.

The chassis ticked and settled for a few seconds. Stillness fell. A truck drove by, slowed, but didn't stop.

The gas station was still at least a quarter mile down the road.

Mindy cursed and banged the steering wheel, then cursed some more as pain shot up from the heel of her hand.

"Fuck, fuck, *fuck!*"

The pain and outburst cleared her head enough for resignation to set in. She picked up the phone first, texting a sad face to Logan. She tapped a finger on the screen thoughtfully, reaching for the proper wording for an apology.

Sorry I'm late for all the kink

Nope, shouldn't focus on the kink, he might not have that in mind right now. Delete, delete, delete.

My car broke down, I'll get there when I can

Too impersonal.

She tried another few things but had arrived at nothing good when a knock on the window scared the phone right out of her hands. She fumbled for it, but dropped it into the foot well, as she turned to see who the *fuck*.

Chet.

She was either the most mortified or the most grateful to see him that she'd ever been to see an officer of the law.

She tried to roll down the window, but the key was turned all the way off. Holding up one finger, she flicked the key halfway, and pressed the button.

He was staring at her through the cop glasses with his judgy frown clearly visible below the mustache.

"Miss Valek."

"Sheriff Garcia."

"It was my understanding you were due at Hilltop by no later than three thirty this afternoon."

She sighed. "Your understanding was correct."

Chet looked at his wristwatch—Mindy found herself faintly surprised he didn't carry an old-fashioned pocket watch instead; it seemed more his speed. "It is three thirty-five. I have also received a distressed text message from my cousin regarding an unwelcome visitor to the ranch."

"What?"

"Explain why you are not where you said you would be. And why you are dressed for business. What are your intentions?"

Just one contraction. She would have thanked him for just a single, solitary contraction, or at least a kind look at that moment. "Well, Chet, it seems that after getting called in to work this morning unexpectedly, only to decide to quit my job because I'm being completely shut out and everything is terrible—and that may end up meaning my mom is gonna disown me—I spend five hours on the road trying to make it to the one place I actually want to be, and ten minutes before I can get there, my car completely falls apart. That's what it felt like, anyway. I tried to turn up the farm road to get to Hilltop, the car wouldn't turn, then it seemed like the whole damn thing fell out a piece at a time and it sounded like I was leaving it all in the road for about a hundred yards or so, and then I pulled over so I could say some curse words at the car because it wasn't *going* anymore, and here you find me. This hasn't been my best day."

His frown deepened. After a second he removed his hat, and bent out of sight. Mindy leaned out the window to see what he was doing. He hadn't gone far, and he didn't stay down long before standing up again and replacing his hat.

"Your story checks out. As least as far as your car is concerned."

"*Ya think?*"

Chet gave a heavy sigh, and his jaw flexed. "You didn't leave any car parts in the road. However, your CV joint is, I believe the mechanical term would be, entirely fucked."

"That sounds bad."

He opened the door for her. "Roll up the window, gather any valuables. I'm driving you to Hilltop."

Chapter Sixteen

When the cruiser rolled up at the back of the short line of cars, Logan didn't even *think* about Chet.

What he thought was, *Great, and now a cop. Just what this get-together needed.*

It was all over. He might as well start packing his bags.

Derek Larch wasn't a bad guy. Not actively evil. He had even been nice enough to come visit Logan in person, because he felt the emails were too impersonal, and Logan had consistently declined to meet with him.

Logan hadn't had time. But Larch didn't know that. And hey, he'd gone to school with this guy. They'd eaten hundreds of lunches in the school cafeteria, eyeing girls and talking about sports. Been on the academic decathlon team together. Even been in the same group to rent a limo for Senior Prom.

Rough as the situation was, Logan almost felt bad for Derek, because more than anybody currently up at the ranch, Derek's hands were pretty much tied. Bud Jameson had him over a barrel—and wasn't that an image Logan wished he'd never conjured.

Bud had been nothing but pleasant to Derek. But Derek knew what Bud was. Everyone did. Everyone knew exactly what Bud wanted, and Derek didn't have a leg to stand on as long as Logan wasn't 100 percent solid on his loan. He'd given Logan all the slack he could, but he wasn't willing to lose his job over it. The time had come. He was selling it off. And he was pretty damn sure the loan service company who was buying it was absolutely in Jameson's pocket.

And those were the breaks. Business was business. And wouldn't Logan rather go up to the house and discuss this in private, rather than out here where these . . . large gentlemen were listening in on every word?

Logan assured Derek this location was just fine. He pretended to listen, and nodded as Derek spoke. His ears were full of static. Because Mindy hadn't shown. And if Mindy hadn't shown, and Derek had, that either meant the whole thing really was a setup, or that Mindy didn't want to be a part of his life after all. And it was clear Bud knew *something* was going down at Hilltop this weekend, or he wouldn't have sent Derek at that particular moment on a Friday afternoon, right?

So ultimately, what Derek said didn't matter nearly as much as the larger question—which would show up next, the law or the press?

He scanned the skies, half-expecting helicopters with cameras.

Up the hill, they'd already started setting up the pony derby area; when he'd last seen the main corral, somebody was already long-lining a pair of nicely matched ponygirls, while two other handlers were gearing up their ponies for a turn in the ring.

They were all so screwed, and he'd allowed it to happen.

And then the police cruiser drove up, the top light clearly visible behind the other waiting cars.

Sure. Of course. Inevitable.

When he recognized Chet, he was a little confused. When he saw Mindy get out the other side, he gave up trying to make sense of any of it.

She was in a suit—or a jacket with a dress or something like that, he couldn't really tell—not dressed for the ranch.

"Your backup's here," he told Derek, interrupting whatever the guy was trying to tell him.

"My what?"

Derek looked where Logan pointed. Mindy walked toward them, waving hesitantly at the giant biker who stepped in her way.

"Name?"

"Mindy Valek. I'm on the list. Logan, what . . . ?"

He considered telling Bloodworm to keep her out, but figured there was no point. Chet was coming in anyway. None of it mattered now.

When she'd been checked off and waved through, she jogged up to him and Derek, doing the awkward high-heel run. He hadn't seen her in work clothes before; she looked a little disheveled, not nearly the crisp office look he would have expected.

Mindy opened her eyes wide at him—pleading, trying to say something without words, he didn't know what. Then she turned to Derek. "Mr. Larch, I'm so sorry you drove all this way. I think my stepfather has been trying to reach you, but your office seems to be closed for the day?"

"We spoke around ten this morning . . ." Larch loosened his tie, looking even more uneasy. "Was there something after that?"

"Yes," Mindy said with a brisk nod. "He found out I was en route and gave me some directives. He wanted to set up a meeting with you for Monday afternoon." She inclined her head toward Logan. "I can't really share the particulars right now. I'm sure you understand. I also have some details to discuss privately with Mr. Hill. About the potential lease agreement they discussed this afternoon, after my stepfather spoke with you?"

Potential lease agreement? What the fucking fuck?

Logan held his hand up. "I don't know what you're talking about, but I never—"

"Right, right." Mindy smiled at them both and shook her head. "There *is* a confidentiality issue, right now, because there's another potential buyer. You're right, Logan, I apologize. We can discuss it at our four-thirty meeting. So glad I made it in time, my car broke down. But the sheriff happened by and was kind enough to offer me a lift."

Chet had walked up behind her. He tipped his hat. "She's going to be needing a new vehicle."

Her car had broken down.

The sad face. It was because *her car had broken down.*

The fog in his brain started to clear.

"Derek, we're hosting a private group here this weekend, as you can see. But I'll be there Monday to discuss the loan with you and Jameson. And Mindy. Right, Mindy?"

"Absolutely." She turned a gorgeous smile on Derek, who smiled back like a man hit with a Cupid's arrow. "It was so great to see you, Derek. So sorry for the mix-up! I'll let Pop know I got ahold of you, so he can stop trying to reach your poor secretary."

Then she said some more things, and eventually put her arm

through Larch's and walked him to his car, still grinning and nodding and being all kinds of charming.

Laying it on a little thick, possibly. But the guy seemed to eat it up. So Logan didn't care.

By Monday afternoon, he'd have all the receipts in order, everything accounted for—or at least enough to bring his payments current and then some. Because things actually did seem to be going according to plan after all. Better than plan.

Mindy had come to the rescue.

"I'm rethinking best practices for how to run a business," Logan said, as he ran the bullwhip over his hand then flung it wide, letting the full length uncurl.

Mindy swallowed and turned her head away, trying not to think about where the whip might land first. "This is probably not the best practice, honestly, sir."

"See, that's where I think you're wrong." He flicked the whip softly, letting it wrap around her calf in a gentle caress. The leather scuffed at her skin as it coiled away again.

She shivered, but not from the cool night air.

"What do y'all think?" Logan asked the small group of onlookers. "Responsible business ownership right here?"

"Responsible some kind of ownership, all right," called a latex-clad top from the row of burlap-covered straw bales serving as a bench.

Mindy and Logan chuckled at the same time. She gripped more tightly at the ropes around her wrists. "Oh, he doesn't own me."

"That reminds me." Logan came up behind her, pressing against her bare back. Rough denim against her butt, his belt buckle a cold note in the small of her back, his chest warm and firm under the thin cotton layer of his plaid shirt. He looped the whip somewhere, possibly over his shoulder, and dug in his pocket for something. "I have something for you. I forgot all about it earlier, with all the . . . excitement."

"Is that what we're calling it?" She tried to press back against him harder, but couldn't get a purchase with her hands secured over her head, limiting her range of motion.

"Shh. Here." He held something in front of her—a black cord with a jewelry clasp. A small cardboard tag hung off it on a ring, cream tag stock with a brown reinforcement around the hole, like something you'd see hanging from a lamp in an antique shop. On one side, it read *Ariel*. Logan flipped it after a second so she could read the other side. *Under the protection of Wildcat.*

His scene name—the term for oil wells that weren't in a big oil field. When he'd told her, she'd laughed until her sides hurt.

He undid the cord and fastened it around her neck, where it hung at the level of her collarbone, with the tag hanging over her sternum.

"Robert said you don't do the leather household thing," she murmured, leaning back to press her cheek against him. The angle was awkward but she needed the contact. "Or collaring." Protection meant different things to different people, but it was still a big commitment, and not one she'd expected.

"Robert doesn't know everything." Logan reached around and fingered the tag, then let his hand drift down to tweak her nipple until she squeaked. "And it isn't a collar." He brushed his lips against her shoulder. "Yet."

She sighed, relaxing into his touch, letting in the pain, but also the affection. Letting in all the possibilities. Her life might be in utter turmoil, but it turned out that this, this one thing, she hadn't fucked up entirely. And it was not a small thing. Only one element was needed to make her night complete.

"Will you whip me with that thing now, sir? Or do I have to beg?"

He chuckled, the vibration running through her whole body. "Let's get this party started."

Chapter Seventeen

Logan reassured Mindy that the former parking lot of the old drive-in wasn't nearly as creepy as she was making it out to be. When they arrived, though, shortly after dark on a Sunday night, he was glad he'd downloaded a backup movie in case *Camp Killsaw 3* seemed too grim for the venue.

He'd been looking forward to a little shrieking and clutching, but Mindy was right—watching a horror flick on the tablet in that empty abandoned lot would have been an open invitation to the mythical guy with the hook for a hand who preyed on young, illegally parked couples in love.

So they spread a sleeping bag and blanket in the bed of Logan's truck, and watched *The Princess Bride* for what must have been at least the tenth time for each of them, and he and Mindy repeated all the same favorite lines and laughed in all the same places and it was pretty much perfect. Except the bagged popcorn they'd gotten at the general store was a little stale.

After the perfect ending, they stared up at the stars, fingers and legs entwined, awash in the smell of old popcorn and bug spray, alive with possibility.

"So I did two things today," Mindy finally said.

"Oh, yeah?" He was expecting to hear something mundane like *laundry and inventory*, because she liked to keep him abreast of that stuff. Or sometimes it was *making the perfect sandwich, all for me, none for you.* Which was fair. Since she was usually telling him via Skype, from her place in Dallas. She had quit her job, but was still technically looking for something else in her own field—though she commuted to Bolero on weekends, and he'd put her on the payroll officially the minute she allowed him to.

"I talked to Mom."

"Oh, shit." He half rolled over, leaning on one elbow to study her face. "How did that go?"

She shrugged. "About as well as you might expect. I don't know. Maybe a little better? I kept worrying that Bud would somehow find out about Giddyup—what it really is, I mean—and that would become a factor, but as far as she knows I'm just making a really questionable career move to leave my secure job with family for some wacky startup dude ranch. That's not quite as bad as 'wacky start-up *kinky* dude ranch.' So she's worried, but more puzzled and hurt than anything else."

"Hurt?"

"That I'd walk away from Bud's generosity."

Ah. So she hadn't had the *whole* talk with her mom. "Are you ever going to tell her about him?"

Mindy shifted her head, looking up at him and lifting a hand to his cheek. "Yes. And soon. But it can't happen too close to the holidays or it'll ruin Christmas. Better to plan on that ruined Christmas starting in summer, than at the last minute, right?"

"Right." He traced his finger over her cheekbone, where the moonlight highlighted the curve. "Do I get to meet her first? Before she knows my full role in the ruination?"

"Yeah, I think you do. Well, and you've already met Bud."

"Maybe a separate meeting . . ."

"Probably better, yes." She patted his cheek, and he started to lean in to kiss her, but she stopped him with a finger to his lips. "Don't you want to know what the second thing is?"

He'd forgotten there was a second thing. He nodded somberly as if he'd been interested all along.

Mindy ran her fingers up into his hair. "You know that little blue house over on Maple that was for rent?"

"Behind the Bewliss's?"

"Yeah. It's not for rent anymore."

It took a second for her meaning to sink in, then Logan grinned. "You're moving back home full-time? Seriously?"

"The lease was almost up on my apartment in Dallas anyway. It was time. So . . . I can actually start doing more at the ranch during the week, instead of trying to cram it all into the weekends when I'm here."

"And . . . you'll be here."

"I hope you can still afford me full-time."

"You know it." He couldn't *not* afford her. She was the idea girl. Not to mention the heart of Hilltop Ranch, as far as the visitors were concerned.

Hell, as far as Logan was concerned.

He reached up to take her hand, pressing it down beside her head and holding it there—pinning her, enjoying the hell out of watching her face shift as she went from talking-about-the-day mode to submissive mode. Ready to give him whatever he wanted—ready to take whatever she needed.

But all they needed right then was a kiss. Perfect and pure.

Robert made the *best* coffee. And he also, it turned out, knew a great deal about inventory management software.

"But I never expected I'd be showing you how to do it. Who would've dreamed . . ."

Mindy highlighted the field he indicated and pored over the pull-down list of categories. "This is the top-level one, and that's . . . consumables, right?"

"Yeah. Not top-level, though, that was what took us to this form. Kitchen. All food goes through the kitchen category, even the stuff for the trail ride cookouts and snacks. *Except* the snacks for sale in the gift shop when we get that set up, that'll be on its own point-of-sale system."

She finished the entry and moved to the next item, which was basically the same except for the amount. "After this you're gonna show me how to generate the shopping list, right? Is it the same for vanilla events?"

"Yeah, the numbers just vary more because we don't always get the cap. No wait list or begging for spots when it's not Giddyup time."

The ranch had settled into a routine: one Giddyup weekend a month, and the rest of the weekends and some weekdays taken up with what a lot of the staff called "vanilla time."

They'd had to let Lamar in on it. To everybody's surprise, the old guy hadn't batted an eye. He'd said something cryptic about it seeming like old times again, and that was that. He'd taken to hanging around the horse barn during Giddyup weekends, talking to the pony players and giving people advice about tack. Next month he was slated to give a daytime talk about proper leather conditioning.

Mindy couldn't get over that this was her job now—this and a hundred other administrative duties at Hilltop. She didn't really have a title—she and Logan couldn't seem to agree on one—but she was definitely making herself useful. For the first time in years, she felt happy with her work. Happy with her surroundings. All it had taken was a lot of trust and a group of kindhearted kinky people with a shared vision for outdoor fun and games.

"You know," she pointed out to Robert, "we really all have you to thank for this. You were the horseshoe nail."

"The what now?" He looked up from his stack of invoices, fluttering his ridiculously long black eyelashes. He looked about twelve; Mindy always had to remind herself he was almost her age.

"For want of a nail, the shoe was lost; for want of a shoe, the—"

"Horse was lost. Yeah, I know the expression, I just didn't know where I came into it."

"Well." She gestured around the kitchen, where she usually sat with her laptop and paperwork on guest-weekend evenings while Robert finished cleaning up from dinner. He no longer did a full dinner on Giddyup Fridays, so tonight he'd had light duty. "It started right here. If you hadn't called Logan "*sir*" that first night, I wouldn't have twigged that he was kinky. I wouldn't have gotten involved with him. We wouldn't have played around on the trails or in the old barn, which got us thinking about how great this place could be for kink. And so on. You were really the magical element. Kind of the— ah, nope. Never mind." She stopped herself, clamping her lips together, but Robert's curiosity was too fired up to let it go.

"*Give.*"

"It's awful."

"Mindy. *Give.*"

"Okay, you were basically the . . . *gayus ex machina.*"

After a second of silence, he clapped his hands over his mouth and started bouncing, paddling his feet in place like a toddler whose Christmas dream had just come true. From behind his fingers a mumbled stream issued forth: "Oh my God oh my God oh my God!"

"That's not offensive? Wait, where are you—?"

He ran past her, still squealing. "I need the desktop computer, I have to go start designing the T-shirt *right now*!"

"But you'll miss the fire lighting!"

"I don't caaaarrreeee," came his reply, dwindling as he turned the corner into Logan's office.

Still laughing, Mindy checked the time then started stacking papers, slipping things back into their folders and tidying everything up for the night. *She* didn't want to miss the fire. It was fast becoming her favorite tradition, and it was nearly time. Guests had started assembling in the yard; the breeze brought her the rising noise of happy voices, the occasional *crack* of a whip or jangle of a harness.

Slipping out the back door, she made her way to the fire pit, where it was easy to pick Logan out of the crowd. He was wearing his black hat, and the dark red shirt she'd gotten him. Black jeans, black boots. Pure Kinky Cowboy. The perfect look for Wildcat, the head of house at Giddyup.

She had on black boots, too, and a wrap dress with a single tie. Nothing else but her cord and tag—which he'd carefully relettered last week in Sharpie, then laminated. At some point, he claimed, he'd have it duplicated in etched silver. She expected she'd see a few other versions before then. Each one a little more permanent than the last. He thought he was sneaking up on her, but he wasn't all that sneaky. Nor did she need him to be.

When the fire went up, the dress would come off. Always a fun start to the weekend. Around October, Logan assured her, he would set up outdoor space heaters so they wouldn't have to give up that part of the Giddyup tradition.

"When Ariel gets naked, the party gets going," he'd told her firmly when she raised the concern. "That's the deal."

"I think it's really when the fire starts, but okay."

He spotted her and held his hand out, and she made herself walk, not run, to his side.

"Accounts all taken care of?" he asked, then kissed her forehead.

"Mmmm. Yep. Just about, at least. Robert was showing me some stuff."

"Awesome. You getting settled in?"

She sighed. "I have the last load of stuff in my car. I hope it'll be okay in the parking lot. I didn't have time to take it all into my house before everybody started showing up. Then I was on show-newbies-to-the-cabins duty."

"It'll be fine. You sure you don't just want to bring it all into *my* house?"

"Logan . . ." Moving to Bolero and taking the job at the ranch had been a big enough step. One day—maybe even one day soon—she would take the next step and move into the big house with Logan. Her boss, her Dom. Her boyfriend, crazy as it seemed. But for right now, she had more than enough change to deal with, and she wanted to hang on to a space of her own just a little longer while she adapted to life back in her hometown.

"Maybe just one box," he teased, plucking her name tag up and giving it a suggestive rub. Or maybe it was his expression that made it suggestive. "As a placeholder."

"We'll see." She already had a small box set aside for that, in fact. But she didn't have to tell Logan that yet. Extra toiletries, a few changes of clothes. It made sense; she was at the main house all the time anyway. "Did you get *your* paperwork taken care of today?"

Big Gerry interrupted them, holding out the tin of fireplace matches. "Hey, boss. It's time."

Logan gave her an apologetic squeeze and took the matches, then went into his spiel for the crowd. Welcoming them for the weekend, giving the thirty-second history of Giddyup, and then striking the match and starting the fire. The usual cheer went up. Mindy fingered the tie on her dress, waiting for his attention. He caught her eye but shook his head. After everybody broke into their separate conversations again, he took the end of the bow between his fingers.

"I *did* get my accounts taken care of today," he told her, grinning smugly. "New loan is a done deal. And it's a fuck of a lot smaller than the old one. For which I have you to thank. Have I thanked you for that today?"

She shook her head, glad the firelight was hiding the blush she could feel. "I'm sure you'll find a way, though."

He nodded and tugged the bow loose, then nudged the dress off her shoulders. Always a gentleman, he caught it before it landed on the ground.

"I have a few ideas in mind," he confessed. "Say, eight o'clock in the old barn?"

"Why, sir. In front of all these people?"

They shared a laugh. Logan reached out boldly, fondling her breast, tracing his fingers over the spot where he liked to leave his mark. "That way they all know how much I appreciate you."

"Eight o'clock it is, then." Mindy shivered in the night breeze, breathing in heat from the fire and the even warmer regard from Logan's eyes. "I'm all yours."

Want more Giddyup?

Keep an eye out for

ROPE 'EM

Available January 2017

From Lyrical Press

ABOUT THE AUTHOR

Delphine Dryden has written contemporary and erotic romance for Carina Press and Harlequin, and mainstream steampunk romance for Berkley Publishing. She has also self-published. Her writing has earned an Award of Excellence and Reviewers' Choice Award from Romantic Times Book Reviews, an EPIC Award, an IPPY Gold Medal, and a Colorado Romance Writers' Award of Excellence. She was the also the inaugural winner of the Science in My Fiction contest. When not writing, she can be found editing for various freelance clients and for Riptide Publishing. Visit her at delphinedryden.com.